The Sunset

(Translation of Original Maithili Novel 'Sooryasta'
by Mayanand Mishra)

Yogendra Pathak Viyogi

First Edition 2025

Self-published with printing on Notion Press Platform
(www.notionpress.com)

Contact : viyogi@gmail.com, +91.9831037532

Second January 1930

It was the usual Sunrise on Earth but in Dharampur village who knew how the Sunset would be? Who would know that the red colour of Sunrise mixed with the red colour of human blood would write what on the terrified night's dark stage? What would be the result of that call of revolution?

Was the result known to William Kutt? Or to his son Peterson? Or to his friends arriving from Calcutta (now called Kolkata)? Or to his daughter Annie?

Annie looked at the wall clock. Exactly eight in the morning. Now she could not stay in bed any longer. The three blankets on her body suddenly felt heavy. Half an hour to prepare; fifteen minutes of walking distance; exactly ten o'clock to the School.

The school was opening today after a week's break. She would not tolerate any changes in the school timetable. No matter how cold it may be, or how heavy it may be raining.

It is cloudy, that she has been watching for the last two hours from the window. And she is also looking at the sweater knitted over the last week, remaining awake through the nights.

The sweater would fit Manik well. Throughout the night she has been keeping that sweater close to her breast. She cannot even recollect how many times she would have kissed that sweater during the nights while taking out the knitting needles.

She also cannot recall when she fell asleep. She had been wide awake for a long while, imagining when it would be daytime, when she would go to school and when she would gift that sweater to Manik. How would he feel? How would the sweater fit him? How would it change his appearance? The face of yesterday's Manik quickly flashed as a rainbow in front of Annie's eyes.

Finding Pincot around two days ago, her bright sparkling eyes had suddenly turned pale and lustreless. Her dazzling face glowing in enthusiasm turned ashen. She knows Manik gets irritated at the very sight of Pincot.

She also used to get irritated with Pincot. That is why she did not complete the knitting on the first of January. Even though she would have liked it very much, she could not give the sweater to Manik on the first day of the year.

She could not give even though Pincot had begged for it; he wanted to wear the sweater knitted with her own hands.

Annie did not want it that way. She only wanted to give that to Manik. She had knitted the sweater for him and him alone. For him alone, she kept awake over nights in order to finish the sweater in time. The sweater wasn't ready yet, but Pincot made his request.

That irritated her very much the day before yesterday, the last day of the previous year, seeing Pincot's shameless, hungry and lustfull face. She felt as if a worm had fallen in a glass of milk or a fly had fallen in a cup of tea. She felt as if a spider was crawling near the corner.

Pincot had entered her room in the evening the day before yesterday. That day just before evening tea, he had arrived with half a dozen friends riding horses belonging to the Collector of

Purnia to celebrate the New Year at Dharampur village in the Bungalow of William Kutt.

The party arrived and the house became chaotic. Everyone trooped in and began creating fuss of all sorts. The last two days were spent in extreme chaos and disorder. The 31st of December of 1929 and the first of January of 1930. The last night of the previous year and the first day of the New Year.

Plenty of drinks, eggs, cutlet, snacks, roasted chicken, *kebab* and meat to eat, vulgar and shameless songs with accompanying loud music. Endless demands to the bearers, servants of all grades and skills running in all directions, bringing food, bottles, glasses and what not. They were by now fed up with these rowdy guests- just half a dozen in the company. Tony and Pit along with the leader Pincot. Mary, Maria and Jennie were the female members of the company.

Poor Mary! She only needs booze, cigarettes and a partner for sex, whosoever that might be. Poor soul! She can manage relationships with half a dozen men at a time. Sex remains at the top of her mind. And for that one needs drinks, cigarettes and men.

Jennie too likes men but she is selective and keeps within limits. She is not drowned in liquor all the time. She does not get sozzled. True, she isn't physically as appealing as Mary. Neither the physique nor the back and also not the front view. Mary is a well-endowed woman, who has a fully developed body with heavy hips and elevated breasts; that readily draws the attention of any man. But Jennie looks a school girl, little, pretty and sweet. Jennie informed that Mary had three abortions lately. That's the reason she looks a little dull.

Mary's story is that of a woman strayed and misguided. Her father, a big industrialist and the cotton king who owns a famous mill – Nelson and Co. - lives in Calcutta. He has a fat bank balance and a large farmhouse. He has his own Industrial Estate in London, a colony in Liverpool, and a powerloom as well in Lancashire.

Mary's great-grandfather Nelson had served the British East India Company government in the olden days. His knighthood was not hereditary. He was just an ordinary lower middle class person. But he, who carried bundles of clothes to hawk around the streets of London, had exceptional business acumen.

London of those days was not like it's today. The town was merely a collection of small hamlets or little townlets. People slept on straw mats. Before 1757 it was agriculture that kept London going.

Nelson ferried bundles of clothes through those localities and was always on a lookout for whosoever might have come from India. He enjoyed listening to their tales. He enjoyed listening to the tales of how India was being plundered, how lavishly the Moghul kings, Nawabs and their minions lived, how the local kings led a opulent life and how their vanity led to fights at the drop of a hat.

But the most he enjoyed was the stories about plunder, also how the European countries, French, Dutch, Portuguese, and British, fought among themselves there. And how cleverly the British were driving others out to plunder India all by themselves! Scores of British were going to India. All these people, poor before landing in India, were returning as super-rich.

Nelson too wanted to be rich. He first transitioned from a small-time agricultural labourer to a cloth hawker in London and elevated his status to a lower middle-income class person.

It was around that time when Robert Clive had returned from India. Robert Clive was credited with establishing the roots of the British East Indian Company by defeating the Nawab of Bengal at Plassey. But in London, his arrival generated enormous controversies. His cunningness, meanness, ways and means of plunder became the talk of the town. Be it the House of Commons, the House of Lords, Buckingham Palace, hotels, pubs, restaurants, on the roads and in the drawing rooms, this was the only topic of discussion, people making him a villain and a fall guy.

He was put on charge and was in great trouble. And it was under these circumstances that Nelson came forward to help him. He served Clive well. Clive was impressed by his dedicated service.

After the dust settled, Clive was honoured with Lordship and returned to India as Governor-General in 1765. He brought Nelson to India with him and appointed him the Dewan of Bengal. Thus Nelson got the opportunity – to plunder – he had only heard about. His fortune began shining like the towers of Buckingham Palace. 12th August 1765 was the day he was appointed the Dewan. That meant he was in-charge of collecting taxes for the Bengal region. That was the result of the kindness shown by Clive.

And because of the same kindness Clive never questioned Nelson about the tax receipts. He would not listen to any complaints regarding the tyrannical behaviour of Nelson in collecting taxes.

As such the tyrannical behaviour was the hallmark of East India Company. Nelson's name created fear among the peasantry and tenants. People used to tremble at the very mention of his name. He used to whip people till they bled all over. Then another person would sprinkle salt over the wounds. It was normal for Nelson to whip people till they fell. Many of them would die.

Nelson used to deposit just one percent of his collection into the Company's account. But because of Clive, no one ever questioned him. His personal wealth multiplied by leaps and bounds. He began his own business even while in the employment of the Company. His business model was based entirely on cheating, deceit and lies. He would make false pretensions to take leave from the Company and visit London once in three years. He would deposit his ill-gotten wealth in India into banks in London. During one such trip to England, he was thrown into the sea by another passenger on the ship.

His son, Nelson II, grandfather of Mary, had taken charge of the business in England. He was knighted because of his wealth and influence. Lord Nelson II had transitioned from the middle class to the upper class in society.

He set up industries in England also. His wealth began multiplying there. This was aided by the Industrial Revolution. James Watt made the steam engine in 1769. Then came the steamship in 1807 and in 1825 Stephenson added another feather in the industrial development by introducing the steam locomotive for trains.

The pace of development of Lord Sir Nelson's industries rapidly picked up. Nelson and Co. became famous. And then the Sepoy Mutiny of 1857 happened in India.

Lord Sir Nelson II showed exemplary courage and bravery during the mutiny. He helped the Company in various ways in their fight against the Indians. He was instrumental in drafting the plans for the suppression of the revolt through the use of cruel means. He was notorious for the atrocious behaviour like his father.

Pleased with his atrocities, Lord Canning, on the advice of the British Prime Minister, appointed him the Resident of Khursan Estate.

After being appointed the Resident, he gave up cruelty and began learning the social practices of gentlemen. Nonetheless, he did not give up deceit, cunningness and falsehood. Using these weapons, he slowly amalgamated the Khursan Estate into the British Indian territory. It is said that the King of Khursan had a very cordial (tending to amorous) relationship with Mary's grandmother. Mary's grandmother used to visit the Khursan King and sometimes Nelson II, her husband, visited Calcutta.

Not only did Mary's grandmother visit the household of the King, she virtually ruled the Khursan Estate. The subjects obeyed her orders. The king would blindly put his seal on whatever she wished. The king would also keep himself absent from the court on the orders of Mary's grandmother.

And in the end, the King got fed up with the daily bickering and on the advice of Mary's grandmother, accepted a pension, decided to live with her in Calcutta and surrendered his Estate to the British.

The assimilation of the Khursan Estate with the British Empire made Lord Sir Nelson famous among the Residents. This was also discussed at length and praised in the British Parliament.

It was during those days that, one night when in a drunken state the king tried to have sex with Mary's grandmother, she hit him so hard in the belly that the king fell down the third-floor window. The next morning newspapers carried the headline regarding the demise of the king of Khursan Estate, Maharaja Thakur Khadga Bahadur Singh, K.C.I., from a fall from the third-floor window of his Bungalow. The Government condoled the death.

Personally, Lord Nelson had no regrets, rather he felt happy and satisfied. Satisfied, because there was nothing left in the treasury. The wealth of the Khursan Estate had disappeared mysteriously. The British Government could not find that out.

The only person having knowledge about this mystery was Mary's grandmother. All her jewellery was made of only diamonds and other precious stones, ruby, sapphire, jade, pearls and what not. Gold was too insignificant an element to adore her body.

Lord Sir Nelson III, later Mary's father, was her only son and heir to unlimited riches, the sole owner of the same famous Nelson & Co. Halo, fame, money, and trust - he possessed all of them in plenty.

But Mary has no peace. She is running after booze, tobacco and men. Poor Mary!

And Pincot is falling for that very poor Mary. He entered Annie's bedroom the day before yesterday - unannounced, drunk, unsteady, and eyes burning in passion.

-"Hello Annie, how are you?".

-"Hi", Annie's reply was cold. She looked at him once with disdain and remained seated on the bed, knitting.

-"Surprising!" Pincot said frustrated.

-"What's wrong?"

-"Wouldn't you invite me to bed?"

-"Why?"

-"For the New Year's kiss?"

-"No, never; don't even dream of it".

-"Why?"

-"You know well, I hate liquor". Annie gave a hard look at Pincot and continued knitting.

-"I am sorry; please forgive me, but what about the New Year kiss?"

Just then the maid entered the room with a castor oil lamp. Seeing Pincot standing there, she kept the lamp in the corner and began leaving the room quickly.

-"Roopy!" Annie looked at the maid with purposeful eyes.

-"Yes, Ma'am".

-"Sit here".

-"Ma'am". And she stood behind Pincot in great surprise. She had been amazed while entering the room. She knew no one entered Annie Ma'am's room, that too a male.

Pincot was a regular visitor to the Estate but he wouldn't ever enter the isolated bedroom. And that too in a drunken state! He knew well that Annie hated liquor. Roopy also was aware, that unlike the intimate relationships among many other male and female members of the White community, the relationship between Annie Ma'am and Pincot was very formal and superficial. She knew too well that Ma'am was different, very different from all other members, male and female, of the British community. Unlike other White members of their society, Annie Ma'am did not drink; she also did not eat non-veg food. She took a bath daily, very much like the Indians. After the bath, she would stand in front of the statue of Jesus Christ and Ramkrishna Paramahans. She would pay her obeisance with folded hands. Then only would she go to the dining table for breakfast.

And for breakfast, she would mostly have fruits and milk, seldom eggs.

-"Are you knitting the sweater?" Pincot tried to be sober even in his drunken state. He had understood why Annie held the maid back in the room. He read her face, studied her posture and drew his own conclusions. He felt uncomfortable even in the drunken state. He felt as if all the happiness of the New Year Eve had been sucked away.

-"Yes, you see it".

-"I am sure this is for me".

Annie kept quiet.

-"I am sure this will be the New Year's gift for me. I am still keeping in safe custody the pen you gifted me last year".

-"Who else has come here?" Annie asked just for formality.

-"Jennie, Mary, Maria, Tony and Pit are there with me, six in all, Maria and Mary first started from Calcutta, then I and Tony joined them in Patna. We four came to the Bhagalpur Collectorate. Took Pit with us and then we all came to Purnia.

There we took Jennie with us and drove here. The road to your place is very bad".

Annie continued knitting silently. Pincot remained standing, feeling very bitter.

-"We have been making the programme through letters since last October. As per the programme, we shall take Peterson along and go to Lahore".... Pincot stated in a somewhat cryptic style.

-"Lahore?" Annie was a bit surprised and asked. She again became silent and continued her knitting. Pincot was still standing, feeling embarrassed. He kept his eyes focused on Annie with that disconcerted look.

-"Yes, we plan to visit the Jaliya Bagh there".

-"It's not Jaliya, but rather Jallianwala Bagh. But what is there to see now?" Even though Annie didn't want to talk, she involuntarily asked.

-"In 1919 a massacre had taken place there. There had been a lot of criticism of General Dyer that he had shot at unarmed people in an enclosed space with no escape. We just want to see the place".

-"Your group doesn't even discuss such topics. Whose idea was it anyway?"

-"Mine".

-"Yours?" Annie was startled. Leaving her knitting for a moment she gazed at Pincot's face. She could not find the burning desire in his eyes anymore which existed a few minutes earlier when he had entered the room. This surprised her further. She didn't expect such a quick change.

Pincot's relationship with Annie is mostly familial, both being from the same family line. Their relationship could be described as brother and sister, albeit distantly. But the two got introduced to each other only in India, in the Wheeler Senate Hall of Patna University on 17th December 1927. It was the tenth-anniversary celebration of the University. Elin, one of the students of that university, had come to know that Pandit Madan Mohan Malviya was to attend the celebrations. She knew that Annie held Pandit Malviya in high regard. Therefore she had informed her about the event and also invited her to attend. Although Pandit Malviya could not come to Patna due to some reasons and the main aim of Annie going to Patna from Dharampur remained unfulfilled, she had a chance to listen to Pincot's lecture there. She came to know that Pincot was a student of the university and also famous for his relations with Mary.

She had been disgusted with Pincot's lecture. The topic of his lecture was to denigrate the Indian civilisation and culture. He had based his talk on the book 'Mother India' by Miss Mayo and even quoted several instances from that book. At the same time, he had concluded that every Indian should be indebted to the British because it was the British who initiated several reformative and new scientific thinking among the Indians.

Annie still vividly remembers how she had become agitated after listening to the lecture. She felt pity about the speaker's ignorance and complete lack of original thinking about the Indian culture and had developed a sort of aversion towards him. It is a different matter that there is a class of British who subscribe to the ideas propagated by Miss Mayo and she detests the entire class.

During that very first meeting with Pincot Annie had developed hatred towards him. The first meeting had actually taken place at the residence of Elin's uncle, where Elin used to stay in Patna and Annie had also stayed with her. Elin's uncle was a senior functionary in the office of the Governor of Patna.

Pincot had also come to the residence of Elin's uncle after the event at the university. There Annie was introduced to him. During that meeting, their familial relations were discussed and

Annie came to know that Pincot was a drunkard, debouch, rogue and insistent character. Whatever she had seen of the unruly and curious behaviour of Pincot towards Mary had filled her with extreme disgust.

Not only had she been disgusted, but she had developed hatred also towards him. Even after knowing the familial relations between them and knowing that Mary was easily available to him, he behaved inappropriately with Annie. Burning with lust, he even attempted to get physically intimate with Annie. Such a behavior had left her stunned.

Later around midnight, Annie had heard tap at her door several times. She had been filled with extreme revulsion towards Pincot. She had a dislike for Pincot's father also, although she had never met him. She had heard so many stories involving the senior Pincot. Stories of debauchery, scandals, and swindling. He is a senior officer in Madras Residency. And getting married and then getting divorced is his passion. He has already had half a dozen marriages and divorces.

Marriage and divorce are routine for Pincot's father - even remarrying the divorced wife only to divorce her again, so much so that this is no longer a topic of discussion within the British society of Madras (now called Chennai).

Not being discussed any more within that society is also the habit of Pincot's father to offer his wives to Indian princes and Nawabs. It was in this chain of marriages and divorces that he came into contact with a German woman. Pincot is the son of that woman. It is said that the woman was an agent of the top German spy agency and she had been killed in an accident during some spying venture.

Pincot does not maintain any contact or relationship with his father. He left Madras and came to Patna because of Mary. His father, however, keeps regularly sending him the allowances for his education.

It is likely that because of all these reasons, Annie does not have a good opinion about Pincot. In spite of all these, she had given several useful suggestions to Pincot in Patna that day at the residence of Elin's uncle after the anniversary function was over. She had told him, "You are a student of History and Eastern Culture. You should not get biased with Ms. Mayo's views about India. A biased opinion leads to the perversion of original thinking. You should study and research in all aspects yourself. Then whatever conclusion you may draw will be much closer to Truth."

Pincot replied in a conceited manner, "If I continue to get your attention, kindness and sympathy, I am sure I shall think positively."

Annie still recalls how she had disliked and hated the tone and tenor of Pincot's impertinent reply. And each time they met, Annie's hatred towards him went on increasing. Once at the residence of Purnia's Collector, Pincot had the temerity to kiss Annie suddenly.

She felt disgusted that day too. Actually, Pincot was under the wrong impression about Annie and this confusion had proved an encouragement for him.

Before that kissing incident, there had been a hunting expedition organised by the Collector of Purnia district. A special friend of the Governor had arrived from Patna. Annie along with Mary was among the group of spectators. Pincot was also part of that party. They were all seated on the same elephant.

During the search for game, suddenly a cheetah attacked the elephant. Although the animal was shot dead just while attacking, it left Annie so terrified that she held Pincot tightly in that state of dread. Using this as a golden opportunity Pincot also tightly embraced Annie. Not only that, he began thinking that Annie had surrendered to him. Even though after this trivial incident triggered by fear-induced agitation, everyone continued watching the hunting of wild animals, Pincot began planning different advntures. This confusion still occupied Pincot's mind.

Looking at today's Pincot, however, Annie was not confused. His eyes were unusually calm and serene, and his face appeared remorseful. He was feeling ashamed, and his appearance asked for forgiveness.

Pincot was still standing. He did not show any impertinence to sit without permission. Even though his mouth smelled of liquor, his actions were not at all unruly. Annie could not comprehend the sudden change in his behaviour.

Roopy was standing silently behind Pincot. She had been watching with surprise the firmness of her Mistress and Pincot's sudden submissiveness and dignity. She was also amazed by the change in Pincot's attitude. A person who was known for singing all the time, creating a ruckus, being uncivil at every step and showing unruly and defiant behaviour had suddenly turned docile like a cat before Annie Madam.

-"Roopy!" Annie just looked at her.

-"Yes Ma'am".

-"Tea".

Roopy left the room hurriedly. She felt so relieved as if released from jail. She failed to understand why she was told to to stay that long. And whatever she could guess turned out to be baseless by finding poor Pincot standing there meekly like a cat. She felt confident that no one with evil intentions could ever dare to look into her Mistress's eyes. How subdued Pincot had become? But Oh, that day... Roopy was ruminating...

That day Pincot came all alone. Master Peterson was away on business somewhere. It was evening time. Cook Rahman prepared tea but neither the bearers nor any of the other servants were there. Actually, whenever Master Peterson goes out somewhere, chaos prevails in the Bungalow. All the servants take it easy; many go out to spend time with their families or friends. That's because the old Master William does not now command much fear among the servants. He hardly ever comes out of his room. Otherwise, Oh my God! Who would have dared go out even for a few minutes? Master William was terror personified.

So it fell on her to serve tea to Pincot. Normally that would not happen as she is the personal maid of Annie Ma'am and her job is only to serve her Ma'am, none else.

So the unthinkable happened that day. Pincot suddenly caught her that evening, almost like a tiger would catch a deer. Somehow with great difficulty and pleading she could release herself from his hold and ran away. But today, he looked like a completely changed man. He kept his eyes closed as if in deep meditation. Totally submissive. Not a trace of his old self of a rogue. Roopy felt as if something strange had happened in the life of Pincot to bring about this change.

-"Please sit down". Annie finally spoke.

Her room is on the remotest side of the Bungalow, in a lonely section. A large window opens in the east, another one in the north. Both are closed at the moment. There is only one cot in the room, and near the eastern window, there is a table. A four-headed lamp filled with castor oil is burning on the table. A chair is kept by the side of the table.

-"Thanks. I thought today you will not at all ask me to sit down". Pulling the chair towards him and making himself comfortable on that, Pincot replied with a smile. His smile today was very different from those on previous occasions. Annie did not doubt that. She asked, "Why?"

-"I have committed three mistakes today".

-"Three mistakes! Fine. Then?"

-"Certainly. Over the last three days in the company of this new year party and a charged atmosphere, I lost control of myself and crossed limits".

-"Limits? Well. So what's the number one?"

-"Entered your room without seeking prior permission".

-"Okay, and the second?"

-"Knowing fully well that you hate alcohol, I have been drinking".

-"And the third?"

-"On the eve of the new week of the new year I caused you unnecessary agitation".

-"How did you know I got agitated?"

-"There are three proofs".

-"Oh three! Tell me what's the first?"

-" I kept standing for the last twenty minutes and you did not ask me to take a seat."

-"Agreed. Now the number two?"

-"You continued knitting with even greater speed without even looking at me".

-"This too is taken. And the third?"

-"And you kept the maid waiting here in this room for such a long time without any reason".

-"Without any reason?" And Annie looked hard at him.

-"Sorry, not without reason. Actually, my condition after coming from the party was far from sober by any measure and I realise you needed to hold the maid here".

-"From without any reason to essential, how come this turnaround?" Annie was startled.

-"Certainly Annie, I could have done anything to you".

-"Anything?

-"Of course". Pincot replied with head hanaging in shame.

-"But you did not".

-"Yes because three things caught my attention just after entering the room".

-"Again three. What a mystery! Or just a coincidence?" Annie became a little mollified after looking at his head hanging in shame.

-"Yes", Pincot replied, with his head bowed down.

-"Number one?"

-"As soon as I entered the room I saw Mother Mary over the window".

-"The second?" Annie was getting amused.

-"By her side, I saw the Indian saint Ramakrishna Param".

-"Not just Param, it should be Paramahans". Annie smiled a little.

-"Ramakrishna Paramahans". Pincot uttered with a somewhat choked voice.

-"And the third?"

Before any reply came, something strange happened that left Annie startled and speechless. Pincot was sitting on the chair with tears flowing from his eyes.

It was hard for Annie to comprehend this transformation. She remained silent and kept knitting. She didn't want to interrupt. Pincot remained as he was, tears streaming from his eyes.

Roopy entered the room, kept the tea on the table and left quietly. But even in that moment, she could see the tears rolling down Pincot's cheeks. She was equally surprised: a person notorious for his unruly behavior and shameless hooliganism having tears in his eyes!

Tears kept rolling, Pincot remained sitting on the chair and Annie kept knitting. A flock of birds flying in the evening sky close to the Bungalow, near the northern window of that room, made some twitter noise, distracting the two for a moment.

The sound of loud ruckus made by the party in the main drawing room could be heard in the room here. The aroma of dishes being cooked in the kitchen was also spreading towards the room. The winter chill of the year-end evening was engulfing the room slowly.

Suddenly Annie was moved by the scene. She removed the shawl from her body and stood in front of Pincot. She asked him, "But why are you weeping?"

She went close to him and wiped his tears. She then pointed to him, "Oh, tea has gone cold."

Just then Mary entered the room. She was also startled. Looking at Pincot she exclaimed, "Oh! You are here? And why do you have tears in your eyes? What's all this?"

Hearing Mary's words, Pincot quickly tried to wipe the tears but could not hide them from Mary's eyes.

-"What happened?" Mary, staggering, just held the shoulder of Pincot and swung herself. Her eyes were red and the smell of liquor from her mouth was filling the room.

-"Nothing serious, just some foreign bodies in the eyes and I had to rub them, so tears came out". Pincot tried to be as normal as possible.

-"Something went into the eyes? Here in such a clean room? And that too was being closed by Annie in this lonely room? Mysterious, very mysterious". Mary tried to stand on her own and looked at Annie.

The hint of sarcasm hidden in the word 'Mysterious' was obvious to Annie. But she kept her calm and told Mary, "You will not understand this at present. You are tired after a long party. You need rest. Please go and sleep".

-"Oh I should go to sleep and leave Pincot with you for the night?"

-"Mary!" Pincot got agitated and told her in a slightly raised voice, "You are being very insensitive."

-"Yes, I am insensitive but you two are probably rehearsing the art of being sensitive here alone in the room".

Now it was Annie's turn. She said, "Mary, you are not normal at all. You had no reason to get agitated in front of my native maid. Your health and mind have gone weak after a series of abortions. You need rest at present." Turning to Roopy, she said, "The tea has become cold. Get another two cups of tea." Roopy left.

Hearing the reproach about abortion, Mary's temper flared up. Accusingly she said, "Oho, now you two plan to spend some more time together over tea! Mother Mary protect both of you. My best wishes for the New Year Annie and have a happy night. Good night." And she left the room.

Annie stood there silently for a while, bewildered and speechless. Pincot sat on the chair staring at the burning wicks of the four-headed castor oil lamp in the room, and kept watching the scene without a word. Although all four wicks were burning, only one burned brilliantly and kept the room illuminated, the other three had become a bit dimmed.

This single wick is Annie in this Bungalow. There is Jennie, Mary and also one Maria from Calcutta. But no one can match the aura and brightness of Annie.

Roopy brought tea in the meantime. She kept the tray at the table and went out.

-"Please take tea". Annie gave one cup to Pincot and sat on the bed with the other cup.

Both of them were sipping tea but none would speak. They were neither looking at each other. The only sound audible in the room was that of sipping of warm liquid which would quietly spread to the outside world and vanish.

-"Annie" Pincot finally spoke after keeping his cup on the table, "Can you forgive?"

-"What do you think?"

-"Beyond doubt. I fully understand that my question is rather absurd".

-"Thanks, but forgive whom? You?"

-"You have already forgiven me. I think you must reckon that".

-"Then who?"

-"Mary".

-"Who is she to you?"

-"Mary... Mary meant to me something in the past ... maybe she may again in future... but for the present, she is just a friend. She will continue to be a friend till I don't have any social relation with her".

-"And are you excited about that?"

-"Had you asked this question yesterday, my reply would have been in the negative. However, today the circumstances have changed just now. In that case, my answer would be in the affirmative. Have you seen the flash of lightning? Something similar has flashed within me all of a sudden".

-"So the circumstances have changed now?"

-"Certainly. See, I had never been this long in your company till this evening. Today during the whole session, I am filled with a sense of responsibility. It is the speciality of the great personalities that make even minions feel great. I am drawn towards that special power and that fills me with a sense of responsibility again. And considering the relation I had with Mary in the past, if she desires, I shall have no hesitation in establishing a formal social relationship with her".

-"Shall have no hesitation, means at present it is not, meaning you are hesitant".

-"No, it all depends on Mary. My willingness solely depends on her approval. But ..."

-"But?"

-"The proposition will not arise".

-"Why?"

-"Mary belongs to a Lord's family. Certainly, she would like to enter a Lord's family and as far as I know, there is some talk already going on with the Maharaja of Patiala. For a while, the son of the Resident had also courted Mary".

-"You know for sure?"

-"Sure".

-"What form did it take?"

-"That no one told me, not even Mary. And I did not probe any further".

-"What is your best guess?"

-"Nothing".

-"Why?"

-"Just by guessing how can I make anyone mine?"

-"Why? Mary".

-"No, Mary cannot be reasoned."

-"Why?"

-"Because Mary is dull and indecisive. She cannot make any decisions in her life. In fact, she does not possess any self. Whatever road one may show, she would take that. She would accept whosoever she may meet on that road. She is a rudderless ship, just sailing with the wind."

-"Shall I speak to her?" Annie looked at Pincot.

-"No", was his curt reply.

-"Why?"

-"I can wait. I am in no hurry. Just her wishes may be my curiosity. Otherwise, I am free. And I want to stay free."

Annie remained silent for a while, thinking something. Then she asked, "Then why do you care if I forgive her?"

-"She isn't the cause of my worry."

-"Then?"

-"I worry because of you."

-"Me? What?"

-"See, Mary came to this Bungalow with me and she entered this room also in search of me only."

-"Why do you assume so? She might have come looking for me as well." Annie smiled a little.

-"Not in this party. You don't fit this group."

-"Why?"

-"You are considered a renegade, rather anti-national."

-"Do you also think so?"

-"Look, you are above all these little characterisations. You are truly a global humanist."

-"I am not, nevertheless I am trying to become one."

-"There is always a road to success in the attempt."

-"Thanks, today I am very satisfied after talking to you. There has been a remarkable change in your attitude. I am very happy with that."

Suddenly, Pincot got up, held Annie's right hand with both his hands, kissed it and lifting it up, he touched it with his head in reverence and then kept it back in her lap, and returned to his seat.

After making himself comfortable he said, "Annie, I was drunk no doubt, however, all was done for the sake of the company here. But I can't recall after how long I had touched alcohol. Now I hardly enjoy it. You have not visited Patna in recent months. I have almost left this company. I don't have much interest in their affairs. I realise I have to study a lot. And a company like this is a hindrance to the study. To top it all, I still remember your words vividly, every syllable of them."

-"Thanks."

-"I am not telling all this to please you. Neither is this any explanation for the changes in my behaviour. This is the plain truth of my heartfelt expression."

-"I understand."

-"Thanks. This time again, I didn't have much interest in visiting Jallianwala Bagh. Had the programme of this trip not been made with consensus, then... then I should have backed out. I am in a wrong company. It's a waste of time. But ... I came to join them after a long time and I must confess I lost control. And I entered your room in that very condition."

-"I know all this and after your statement, I became more relaxed. But what is the curiosity regarding Jallianwala Bagh?"

-"Nothing specific, just a sudden curiosity. In fact, the Bagh massacre has become a blot on the entire English race which can never be forgotten in history. Hence I wanted to visit the place and familiarize myself."

-"Your very intent had made me change my views about your behaviour. And the way you wept, your tearful eyes. That, I saw as your remorse."

-"That's true. There was something more."

-"What else?"

-"I entered your room without permission and I received your snub. I felt angry with myself but it had a sobering effect. I found the effect of liquor subsiding suddenly. Yet you looked at me once and continued knitting. ... I became impatient and felt cut off. I became conscious of my irrelevance in my own eyes. I looked at you again. Your face reflected unwavering peace like the sky, extreme firmness like the earth, brilliance like the midday Sun, shining aura like a rainbow, melting like butter, uncorrupted, innocent, and unblemished. For a moment you looked so serene, soft, and sweet. Believe me, I am telling the truth. Your face looked very sweet. I felt as if I was seeing you for the first time in my life." Pincot became silent for a moment, looking at Annie, who was sitting on the bed, her body covered with a shawl, busy knitting. Then he spoke again, "Something surprises me very much."

Annie left knitting. She had been listening to Pincot all along and occasionally casting a glance at him. He was engrossed in his talk and she was listening attentively. She also kept looking at the knitting needle.

True that she was looking at the needle but her entire consciousness was directed towards Pincot. Even though not directly looking into his face, she kept absorbing each word he spoke in its full intent and also kept absorbing the unblemished rays emanating from his posture. She felt that Pincot's entire gaze was focussed towards her face throughout, making it soft and wetting it, touching each vein, each line of her body and it was getting drenched in peace because of the new achievement, attaining happiness and contentment.

She did not want to disturb his satisfaction and the recent change, so she kept quiet even after listening to so much praise from him. The same praise by the same person she would not have liked to listen to earlier at all. But today's Pincot, more so the person in front of her at that moment, was not the person she knew. He was a changed person, new and different.

The sudden mention of surprise by Pincot disrupted Annie's thought process. She looked at him and asked, "What surprises you?"

-"I felt it earlier..." Pincot now removed his gaze from Annie's face and fixed it on her fingers. He kept looking at the needles trapped among the fingers. Then he said, "Felt as if I was seeing you for the first time. Before this meeting, I had never looked carefully at you, as if you did not exist then. I could not recognise you in the true sense. Today I find you completely different and novel."

-"What is surprising in that? Novelty is not within me but in your perspective. That is your new achievement."

"Wait...Wait..., It's this, certainly, it's this", suddenly Pincot said cutting her short, "I had this new perception quite accidentally and miraculously."

"This is not totally new. It happens. It has happened earlier too, even in science. There have been many scientists who were doing something but accidentally discovered something totally different and novel. You must have heard about Newton's story of falling apples. That gave the world a novel law of gravitation, the world was mesmerized. Generally, people consider such things as accidental but I do not completely agree. The thought process in its development takes a definite shape only in steps, and sometimes the path in between is also filled with equal importance which may surprise the person who was developing his thought. This transformation cannot be called completely accidental. The emerging thought process certainly has a root somewhere, a direction also, although not apparently vivid."

Suddenly Pincot stared at Annie's face. He said, "True, it had a root. The thought process had a definite direction. Do you recall our discussion about Miss Mayo after the tenth-anniversary event at Patna in December 1927?"

-"I do recall some but not all."

-"I also do not remember all. But I remember one important thing you told. You had told me about self-analysis. It hurt me somewhere that day. It didn't remain as such, nor was I aware of it always. Today I realised it was not totally dormant, and had been slowly shaking my conscience."

-"Not completely unimaginable. But – a question..."

-"What?"

-"Was remorse the sole reason for your copious tears?"

-"I am just about to describe that. I have no memory of my mother. Just a small hazy picture I recollect. That was my mother sitting and knitting. That is the only recollection I have. And when I saw you sitting and knitting, my mother's picture suddenly came to my mind. That's why I could not control myself. But tears did relieve me. It was good. At one time I thought that I should be sitting by your side and keep weeping indefinitely."

-"I was amazed at first to see you weeping. But when I looked into your face, I became confident. It felt good. But you were telling something regarding your mother. Don't you feel cold? Cover yourself with this blanket and come, sit on the bed."

Saying this, Annie brought a blanket kept underneath her pillow and extended her hand towards Pincot.

Pincot took the blanket and covered himself but did something entirely unexpected: although Annie had shifted herself a little and made space for him on the bed, he did not sit there. Instead, he sat on the floor, just holding Annie's feet.

Annie was shaken and aghast. She exclaimed, "Oh what is this?"

-"I have done just right. Don't move, be seated as you are. Let me sit where I am".

-"But why? What makes you do what you are doing?"

-"The Indian style of sitting on the ground. As we are in India, I follow the Indian custom. You are a great fan of the Indian way of life, aren't you?"

-"Yes, I am, but that does not mean ... dirty..."

-"Dirty? The room is clean, the floor is clean too. ... Oh, I see you are you afraid of the blanket becoming dirty?"

-"Do you think it is a question pertinent to you?"

Pincot raised his head and looked at Annie. Her face indicated a mild indignation. As a result, her lower lip trembled a little.

Pincot found that lovely. He felt an urge to kiss her. Without much thought and still covering his body with the blanket, Pincot held her one foot by both hands and pressed it hard. Then he spoke, "I accept my mistake, please forgive me. I reckon this is the Indian way of asking forgiveness".

-"Fine, but leave my foot."

-"No I shall not for the moment."

-"Why?"

-"It feels better like this." Pincot had the sensation that the entire existence of Annie, her personality, the entire dignity, her entire pleasantness had descended in her foot. So he put his left palm below the foot and with his right hand began caressing it. While doing so, he told her, "I really find peace in doing this. I get unimaginable pleasure."

-"May be you find pleasure but ..." She quickly took his both hands in her hand and lightly pressed them. "What will others say if anyone were to see us like this?"

-"And you were telling me to sit on the bed with you, imagine what would have been the effect of that?"

Within the next instant, waiter Dinu entered the room with the tray, and Roopy followed behind with two glasses filled with water. The scene left them dumbfounded. It was unimaginable for them to find a man in Ma'am's room and that too sitting on the ground. Dinu could hardly utter, "Tiffin, Ma'am".

Annie was still holding Pincot's hand. She told him to move to the table for the Tiffin. She herself just slid a little on the bed to reach the table.

Dinu had already kept the tray on the table; Roopy also kept the two glasses and began serving. Pincot said, "I shall not move, I shall have the Tiffin here sitting on the ground, pure Indian style."

-"What has happened to you?"

-"What happened to me? Many things have happened. What I have achieved this evening here, if the concept of rebirth of Indian philosophy is true then it is enough for my next half a dozen rebirths."

-"Public display of one's accomplishments and arrogance is not considered good in Indian tradition."

-"That you have to teach me. I have accepted you as my Guru."

-"But if I refuse to take the role of Guru?"

-"Then I can always resort to non-violent disobedience, Satyagraha, as followed by M.K. Gandhi."

-"Too much of tall talk! Ok, let's finish the Tiffin first."

-"But I shall take it right here, sitting on the ground." Saying this, he sat cross-legged very much like Indians do. "Annie, please sit down on the ground with me." Pincot requested.

-"This is too much." She smiled and looked at Dinu. She asked him to spread a blanket on the ground for her. She had seen Manik sit on the ground on a blanket while eating. She had thought of giving it a try but didn't get a chance. She smiled and looked at Dinu.

Dinu was overwhelmed. He had never seen an English gentleman and a lady sitting on a blanket on the ground while eating. He felt very happy and ran outside to get a blanket.

Roopy was totally at a loss. She did not understand anything and whatever she could guess, she could not find any meaning to that. She couldn't reconcile with Pincot, an arrogant, quarrelsome, haughty and drunkard, sitting in that room. She could not understand their talking in English but she could still make some sense from their expressions. And whatever she could make out filled her with utter surprise.

In the mean time Dinu brought the blanket and folding it into two, spread it on the ground. Pincot again invited Annie to sit on the blanket.

-"I am fine here, you sit down there in perfect Indian style."

-"I find that you have been possessed by the ghost of Indian style in day-to-day life." Saying this, Annie was beginning to think about going to sit on the ground but suddenly there was an interruption. Taking a cue from Pincot, Dinu quickly folded the blanket again and made a smaller mat-like 'Aasan'.

Annie remembered that she had seen Manik sitting on a similar *Aasan*. That made her happy. She sat down. His entire existence and personality came alive in her imagination. She found immersed herself in his memory to an extent.

Soon she returned to the reality of the present and found Pincot removing certain items from his plate.

-"What happened now?"

-"Just now you mentioned the ghost of Indian tradition."

-"So?"

-"That's why I decided to eat only those items which you eat, nothing else." Now Annie realised that her plate consisted of only one tomato sandwich, a few pieces of cake, some five pieces of boiled potato with a sprinkling of salt and pepper, another plate with two rosogollas, a cup of milk and a glass of water. On the contrary, Pincot's Tiffin consisted of several plates, having a couple of chicken legs with gravy, kebab, and korma in the third, some pieces of cutlet in the fourth, eggs in the fifth, a few rotis in the sixth and the seventh had cut pieces of apples, and then a cup of milk and a bowl of soup.

-"It's fine, why are you hesitating?"

-"No, this isn't fine. From today, I have turned a strict vegetarian, like you."

-"Like me? What does that mean? Now you are bothering people here."

-"Oh, if I bother them then why don't you drive me out? If the Indian hospitality culture permits it, I shall instantly leave this room."

-"Oh, again Indian culture, repeating the same words: Indian culture, are you getting mad?"

-"Ha ha, not getting mad, say gone mad. What's the cure?"

-"Yes there is a cure but..." Annie looked at Roopy again and hinted, "Take back all those stuff and bring the same items as mine for him too. And what about the Tiffin for the other guests?"

-"They had their Tiffin", Roopy answered politely.

-"Where are they?"

-"In the large drawing room."

-"Who are around?"

-"The visitors along with Peter Master and our old Master. ... Old Master has taken too much drink and is just lounging on the sofa."

-"And the others?"

-"Singing, dancing, eating, drinking. Mary is also heavily drunk. She quarrelled thrice with Jennie. No one is listening to anyone. Everyone is only telling his or her part."

-"Oh! Total anarchy!" Annie exclaimed after looking at Pincot and then asked Roopy again, "Who are there to serve?"

-"Everyone from the head chef to bearers, both the peons of Peter Master and Old Master, orderlies, Mangali the spice grinder, the three cleaners, Manager Mr. Sanyal, Deputy Manager Mr. Singh, the accountant Mr. Giridhari Das, everyone, literally every employee of the Bungalow who is able to walk. Just the Gorkha security guard is at the gate."

-"What? The attendants are four times the number of guests. Ok, first go and bring fresh Tiffin for Pincot."

Roopy left the room but Pincot continued looking at Annie. "What are you looking at?" Annie asked.

-"I really don't know.... But frankly what I am getting is so wonderful, so unimaginable and so unforgettable..."

-"But", Annie smiled a little, "looking at a woman like this is considered bad manners."

-"Two points to note – First, I don't consider you just a woman - when I entered the room today till that time, yes, I did think of you only as a woman, an ordinary woman like Mary, Jennie..."

-"My God!" Annie laughed and looked at Pincot, "So if not a woman then what? A man?"

-"No. Neither a man nor a woman, in reality, you are a special specimen of human consciousness, a great creation, the nectar of nature, or better still, the essence of that nectar's sweetness, infinite gratification, inestimable stillness."

-"You are becoming so poetic now!" She again smiled.

-"Poetry is the rhythmic expression of truth; it's a painting of pure beauty, an establishment of Shiva... So what's wrong with it?"

-"Something in your head!" Annie blushed and lovingly shook Pincot's nose. She got up and told him, "Let me spread the blanket further and come near me. The floor is cold."

-"I don't feel cold but anyway, I should obey you. Leave all this mat and space for me and you please move to the cot as before. Please do; that's my wish."

Annie obeyed and sat on the cot. Both of them wrapped themselves with blankets as the room had become quite cold by then. Annie's appreciation of Pincot had increased manyfold.

Pincot continued to sit on the mat and asked, "Should I eat your share of the Tiffin in the meantime?"

-"Oh yes, please do. I am so sorry not to have asked you, you must be feeling hungry as well. Why has Roopy been delayed, I wonder."

-"Very nice, and think of it, a guest has to submit to what the host tells or does to him." With this Pincot gave a hearty childlike laugh.

-"Sorry, it was my mistake." Annie was very apologetic.

-"No problem. When you did not tell me for twenty minutes to sit down, why talk about this small matter?"

-"That Pincot was different. I should never have told him to sit down."

-"And to this Pincot?"

-"No need to elaborate, you see for yourself. Please go ahead and start eating. I still wonder how suddenly you picked up so much of Indian traits."

Pincot did not reply immediately. He began eating avidly as if he had been hungry for several days. Annie was looking at his way and speed of eating. Pincot started again, "Just after the event where I had an encounter with you in the Wheeler Senate Hall in Patna...."

Just then Roopy entered with a tray and was surprised to see Pincot already eating. She was at her wits' end. She could not make out anything about what had been happening.

-"Annie, I cannot explain to Roopy, she will not understand my language. Kindly tell her that whatever she had brought for you and has just brought for me, she should bring three times more."

Annie got up, took the tray from Roopy's hands and transferred everything to Pincot's plate. Then she gestured to her to bring some more.

Amazed, Roopy ran to the kitchen. Annie sat on the cot and Pincot continued eating but asked, "Annie, all this stuff is vegetarian, right? Nothing non-veg. for sure?"

-"Yes, all this is meant for me, I don't eat non-vegetarian food at all."

-"Annie"

"Yes"

-"Should I tell you something? This day will remain an unforgettable day in my life. A day of great happenings. Really, although I don't know in which auspicious timeframe was this trip arranged; if I hadn't come here, no one could have imagined the nature of future Pincot... . Oh no, you again served me your share of the Tiffin, ... I am really doing great injustice to you, please take this for the time being." He got up and handed over the plate containing cakes to Annie.

-"Thank you", and without any fuss, she began eating cake.

-"I have taken many different varieties of food on many different occasions. But the taste I am getting today is unique and mouth-watering. Can you tell me why?"

-"No, better you tell the reason. I am sure you will say something extraordinary."

-"Sure I shall tell. First of all, this mat and the food were for you. Not only this, you had almost sat and were about to start eating. But see I am sitting here and eating food which was meant for you."

-"It's alright, this is only at the emotional level. But it's also true that once you start taking such food on a regular basis, after some time you will begin enjoying them."

-"Already enjoying."

-"It is not as much the taste as how hungry you are that matters. You are really hungry.... When did you start from Purnia?"

-"Eight O'clock in the morning. The party had planned to have lunch here but we were delayed on the way. Mary vomited thrice during the road trip. Once in the midst of fields, we had a drinking session as well. Pit suddenly began beating one of the cowherds mercilessly, but somehow Jennie saved the boy."

-"Why?"

-"He asked the boy about the distance to this place. The poor chap didn't understand the language."

-"So what was the fault of the boy?"

-"None, just that Pit was drunk."

By that time Roopy again entered with more food. Some of the items she spread for Annie Madam and with the rest she sat down near Pincot's mat so that she could keep filling his plates whichever would become empty. She had brought enough provisions for at least two helpings.

-"No, no more. Enough. Nothing more I desire." Pincot looked at Roopy and said, "Thank you Roopy."

Roopy didn't say anything but she understood the gesture. She looked at Pincot once and served him a little of all the stuff. Pincot was surprised, He looked at her with attention and thought the girl was amazing. He told Annie, "India is a marvellous country. Kindly explain to her that I am full of praise for her. She looks adorable. And please also ask her to forgive me for my earlier misconduct." He began eating again.

-"Is it necessary to seek forgiveness?" Annie asked.

-"Yes, very much. It's likely that it may not be necessary for the society to which she belongs. Before today, even I had not cared to seek forgiveness. But today I certainly feel it's absolutely necessary. It's another matter that even if she forgives me, I shall never pardon myself for the abominable act that evening."

Annie didn't say anything. She just watched Pincot's bright face which was grave with the radiance of truth and ... with the sense of responsibility. She replied, "Fine, I shall explain to her."

Roopy didn't understand what was going on but she could guess that they were talking something about her only. She could also make out that Pincot today had been talking of good things, that there was a huge difference between Pincot of earlier times and today's Pincot. She collected all the empty plates and went out of the room.

The room was suddenly filled with the foul smell of alcohol, smoke of cigarettes, and the loud sound of the gang which had assembled in the house on New Year's Eve. Mary, Jennie, Maria, Tony, Pit ... means the entire gang.

All were frenetic, uncontrollable and unsteady.

Mary said, "See the drama".

But they couldn't belive their eyes as they entered the room. Annie was on the cot, Pincot sitting on a mat on the ground. Both of them eating.

-"God save the King!" Tony exclaimed, "Oh Pincot, what's this? You are eating here and that too drab vegetarian stuff?"

-"And that too in pure Indian style", Pit supplemented sarcastically.

-"Like an Indian Yogi" added Maria.

-"You are not speaking anything, Pin?"

-"What do I say? You see what's it here and it's all real as you see." Pincot replied.

-"Each time we made a drink for you, each one of us by turns took it in your absence."

-"I gave up drinking."

-"Since when? You had a drink today for sure."

-"Yes during the day, I gave up drinking this evening."

-"Sure?"

-"Yes, hundred per cent sure."

-"And this vegetarian food?"

-"Yes, now I have become a strict vegetarian. I shall consider myself lucky by becoming a disciple of Annie."

-"What do you say Annie? Have you made him your disciple?" Tony asked.

-"I don't make anyone a disciple. If anyone wants to become one, I only assist him and give him support."

-"Good support! Everything under cover, right? As the Indians say - drinking ghee under a blanket." Mary made a cheap sarcasm.

Annie gave a hard look at Mary and said, "It would have been better if you people sat in the drawing room itself. I am taking food. How long will you all stand here?"

-"Thanks", Jennie replied, "Please don't take Mary's comments seriously. She is not her normal self at present. She has quarrelled with me thrice today. You finish your meal and then come there. Now we have the dance waiting. That should be the finale for the end of the year. And please note, you will have to dance today Annie."

-"I shall have to dance? But I don't know how to dance."

-"Whatever it could be. Please do come to the main drawing room." Saying this Jennie collected the party and left the room.

Turning back Maria asked, "Will you come or you both will go to bed?"

-"Both mean what?" Annie questioned.

-"You and Pincot"

-"Why? Do you need Pincot for yourself?"

-"Your brother is there for me."

-"Then you go, you don't have to worry about me in my house." Saying this Annie pinched Maria's cheeks lightly and funnily pulled them. They all left.

-"Why are you holding your head down, Pincot?" Annie smiled.

-"No-no, I am eating, but what about Guruji?"

-"What Guruji? Who is your Guru? Me?"

-"Certainly. Do you have any objection?"

-"Yes, many objections."

-"But I am not giving you the right to object."

-"Do you have the right?"

Pincot kept his head down till then. He raised it now and looked at Annie. She was composed, loving and smiling.

-"Didn't have but now I have acquired it. Am I correct?"

-"You can decide best for yourself. But remember that rights and duties always come together."

-"I have read it, but henceforth, I shall remember it for life, at least as an instruction from the Guru."

-"Fine, but you should look for a proper Guru. ... yes, you were telling something."

-"I said culturally we are very poor. The Indians are enlightened, humane and liberal."

-"Do you feel that way?"

-"Yes, very much. Whomsoever among Indians I have met and whatever little their literature I have studied, those experiences reaffirm my notion. Don't you see?"

-"What?"

-"Their heightened enlightenment is reflected even in their struggles."

-"What's that?"

-"Think of this. There have been struggles in many places in the world throughout history. It was held in England in 1688, in the United States of America in 1776, in France in 1789 and here it is an ongoing struggle. But tell me do you find here in their struggle the type of barbarism and insolence encountered in other places? No, there is always a measured response and decency in everyone's behaviour. Think of M.K. Gandhi, how polite and patient is his response. Even a furious person like Jawahar Lal Nehru shows enormous patience and humility. To talk of Surendra Nath Banerjee, how much has he been tortured? But did he cross limits? Look at Lala Hardayal of Gadar Party, Tilak.... Strange are these people. Come what may, they never shed their humility and decency."

-"It seems you have studied a lot in recent times."

-"Not much, but yes, I am trying. After the discussion with you at Elin's residence in Patna, I began introspection and that led to my own studies. That's why I consider you as my Guru. You only guided me to the right path of self-exploration."

-"Then why did you come here the way you did earlier in the evening?"

-"Can't say for sure, but most likely the result of that evil company".

-"I also think it could be the result of evil company. But then how can you save yourself from that?" Annie began watching him.

-"You probably don't know about a major incident today. Hopefully, from now onwards it should not make any difference to me, only time will tell. However, let me tell you my future plan."

-"Later, first tell me do you need anything more to eat?"

-"No, nothing, I am full. But tell me, was it a Tiffin or a full meal?"

-"What do you think?"

-"I felt it was dinner."

-"Let that be so." Annie laughed.

-"But actually it was Tiffin time." Pincot also laughed.

-"Then let it be Tiffin only."

-"But I am full. Okay, but you have taken so little. Would that do?"

-"No, I shall take dinner."

-"What will be your dinner?"

-"Pure Indian fares, rice, dal, vegetables, curd, ghee."

-"Then I will also take, but when?"

-"Just at quarter to twelve we sit for dinner, finish by twelve."

-"Can't you make it a little earlier? We should be ready to welcome the New Year sharp at twelve."

-"Fine, eleven-thirty."

-"Good, by that time I should also regain my appetite. Tell Roopy about me also." Pincot looked at the wall clock. It was only 9 in the evening. He left the room.....

*

The train of thought Annie had was broken when suddenly Roopy entered the room and opened all the windows. Annie looked at the wall clock, nine. Oh, bright sunlight. But till an hour ago, it was still misty and cold, cloudy as well, Annie had been watching. She hurried from bed and asked the maid, "Why didn't you come earlier and remind me about the school?"

-"You slept quite late last night. I was afraid it might irritate you."

-"Oh no, I was just lying and thinking over the events of the last two days. Anyway, tell me, is the bathroom ready?"

-"Yes, Ma'am. "

-"What about the members of the party? Has anyone woken up?"

-"No Ma'am, everyone is sleeping, it's very quiet in the Bungalow."

-"Okay, hurry up." She got up and left the room.

Annie quickly got ready for the school. Punctuality was her hallmark. She would not tolerate any disruption in her school routine.

Oh, she recalls, how much she had to struggle to start this school! Opposition from every quarter at every step. Opposition from the Muslim Madarsa, opposition from the Tola[1] Sanskrit Pathashala run by Pandits, opposition from the society against English teaching, and opposition from every guardian against education to the girl child. She cannot forget anything.

She also remembers the overwhelming support of Manik, his encouragement, his talk of giving her the company till the end, his words of comfort, explaining that a project of this nature was bound to generate opposition, but a true leader should also have plenty of courage, perseverance, self-confidence, firmness and also have plenty of good arguments to convince people from all walks of society.

____

[1] _Tola :_ part of a village, a hamlet or a smaller cluster of houses, most likely belonging to a particular caste or community of people. Words like Brahman Tola, Rajput Tola, Musalman Tola etc. are commonly used. Some Tolas, like the Chamar Tola etc are also refered to as 'Chamartoli'. For Musahar Tola a special name is 'Musahari'.

41

That day she had been sitting alone in the school in a state of complete hopelessness. Tired, sad, frustrated and shattered. There was no one around. Just one person, Gopal, the school caretaker also sitting on the veranda in a state of despair. On the campus grass in front of her chair was Tiger, panting and with tongue wide open. The evening was slowly descending.

Oh, she would remember that evening throughout her life. A really memorable one. That very evening Manik had for the first time lifted her by holding both arms and shaking her wildly. The softness, the affinity and the firmness of that touch can anyone forget ever!

Manik had come to school and before Gopal could fetch a chair, he just sat there on the green velvety grass. Annie could not remain seated on the chair and she also sat on the grass. She felt comfortable – sitting with Manik on the soft grass. She had felt relieved seeing Manik at that moment of despair.

-"Why were you sitting all alone here? What were you thinking? Any problem?"

-"Oh, problems galore."

-"Because of me?"

-"Oh no, certainly not because of you, but because of the attitude of the villagers."

-"Rest assured, we shall overcome all the obstacles. In any social and community work, obstacles do come. In reality, you must realise that social and community work is to bring everyone to a minimum point of agreement by listening to everyone and removing their doubts one by one in the first stage. This is certainly difficult and laborious as well, both in physical and temporal terms. A volunteer taking up social work must possess patience and loyalty."

-"Do you have any doubt in my loyalty?"

-"Who says so? I am always praising you. If you had not possessed loyalty towards this goal, and firmness of attitude, certainly you would not have to quarrel with your father and brother for land, for money, for furniture and all that."

-"You know well that I got first strong opposition about this project within my house itself, from my father and my brother. But I persisted. Argued in favour of society, and children's future. And finally, they agreed to support me in principle. Only in principle. The problem of land, money for building construction all that remained. When my father agreed to give a piece of land, there was no money to construct the building. For a long time, the project seemed to be a non-starter. But slowly Father opened his purse as well. I had to plead with them day in and day out, sometimes pretending to be angry with the entire family."

-"I know everything, the day-to-day happenings, the moves and counter-moves, all in vivid detail. And in the end, it is the result of your perseverance, dedication and selflessness that we have the school with the building standing today."

-"But what with the building if there are no students? No guardian wants to send his child here."

-"That will also be solved. Students will surely come. In this connection, I have made some plans. Let's move, it is already evening. We shall win. But ..."

-"But what?

-"What had you been thinking all this while alone?"

-"I had been thinking about you only."

-"About me? What?"

-"That you did not come for the last two days. I don't know what to do next. I have been dependent on you. The amount of help and support you have provided."

-"Oh, don't talk about this again and again. I feel ashamed at hearing this from you. You don't realise that whatever you are doing is actually my job, my village's job. This is the work for the whole society. In effect, you are doing a great national service to Indians."

And suddenly in a fit of emotion, Manik held both hands and lifted her from the ground. He then added, "Let us go, it's evening now. No point in sitting here. All the problems will be solved. It has to be solved. Everything will follow as per your wishes. No power on earth can stop that." There was confidence in Manik's words. Tiger took the lead and the two followed the pet and came out of the school compound. ....

Annie got ready and before departing she went back to her room and lifted the sweater lying on the cot. Then she kept it back on the cot. Kept it and began to walk towards the school. Again she stopped, went back to the room, and lifted the sweater again. She kept looking at it for a while. There was a flash of Manik's face in her mind. She was startled.

Suddenly she heard a commotion outside the door. She kept the sweater back and came out. There she saw Pit, Jennie and Peterson together, looking worried.

-"Annie, did you see Pincot anywhere?" Pit asked her.

-"No, why? What happened to Pincot?"

-"He is nowhere to be found."

-"Means what?"

-"Means that he is not to be found anywhere within this premises."

-"Then where is he?" Annie got worried now.

-"That is what we came to ask you. We thought he might be with you."

-"No, he didn't come here." Saying this she suddenly entered her private drawing room. There is a room adjacent to her bedroom where her clothes and other sundry items are kept. Then next to that room is a room containing cupboards full of books. That is her private drawing room.

Pincot had been sitting on the carpet in this drawing room yesterday for a long time and browsing the books. Annie quickly went to see there, although the chance of finding him there after so many hours was slim. The room was empty, no one was around.

She felt at a loss. She turned to the others and asked, "Did you people check every corner of the Bungalow?"

-"Yes, everywhere."

-"In Peterson's wing?"

-"Not there." Pit replied.

-"In Peterson's drawing room?"

-"No, not at all."

-"Fine, what about any of the guest rooms?"

-"Not there either."

-"What about the backside of the kitchen, where peons and guards live?"

-"We looked every nook and corner."

Annie felt worried and very anxious. She asked, "Then?"

-"That's how we had come to ask you."

-"Yesterday he was with me till about ten in the night, had dinner with me and then he left. Where did he go after that? Did anyone see him?"

-"This I can tell. He came to the main drawing room with a blanket wrapped around him." This was Jennie's statement.

Mary interrupted, "Since the night of 31st December he was seen wrapping himself in a blanket in pure Indian style, like Indian sages, like M.K. Gandhi does."

Mary suddenly became grave and tears began rolling out of her eyes.

-"Mary, don't create a scene. This is not the time to shed tears. We all should put our heads together to search for him."

-"What shall you think?", Mary continued weeping, "It was good for you that he left this place."

-"What do you mean?" Maria was calm and composed, "Why do you think I shall feel good about it?"

-"Sure, you will feel happy. You were the one who teased him always."

-"Me?"

-"Yes, you. You alone. I can say emphatically. During the night of 31st December, you teased him again and again to dance. You only objected to his eating vegetarian food. You were so sarcastic about the Indian ways he had adopted. ... I am sure he left because of you."

-"Mary", Maria drew a long puff of the cigarette she had held in her hand and said, "Frankly Mary, I believe he left only because of you."

-"Because of me?"

-"Yes, because you were always sticking to him and never allowed him any free time."

-"Maria, you are crossing limits. Everyone has seen that over the last 25-30 hours how many times you commented on his newly adopted Indian ways, you almost became hostile about that."

-"That means you had been constantly watching me all along. Mary, actually this is your jealousy speaking."

Annie was getting impatient. She finally addressed both of them, "How long shall we have to listen to your bickerings? Have we gathered here for this?"

Now it was Mary's turn. She accused Annie, "Frankly I am of the opinion that Pincot ran away from here because of you."

-"Because of me?"

-"Yes, yes, because of you."

Peterson intercepted, "What are you people quarrelling about? We have gathered here to discuss where and how to find Pincot. He was our guest here. Let us go in the sun and discuss calmly the issue at hand."

Everyone agreed and they quickly moved to the lawn where some chairs had already been kept. Jennie and Peterson moved in front and Mary along with Annie followed.

Mary whispered to Annie, "You see now, Jennie is getting close to Peterson."

Annie laughed, "So why should I worry or even you are getting jealous?"

-"Am I jealous?"

-"May not be, but the way you behave, people can easily jump to the conclusion that you are always jealous of anything and everything. Anyway, let me ask you something important."

-"What?"

-"Did you say anything to Pincot in the night or yesterday?"

-"No, nothing at all."

-"Then what is your guess of his disappearance?"

-"I don't have a lead, can't guess."

Suddenly Annie stopped and told Mary, "Please continue, I shall be back just in a moment. I have to send an application to the school." And pushing Mary forward she took an about turn and went to her room.

She sat on the chair, took a paper from the drawer and began writing the leave application for the day. But she held back after finishing halfway. She began thinking, "This evening we have a plan to go to Pandit Tola. I have to finalise the programme with Manik. I must go to school even if late."

She just tore the application and returned to the lawn where others were still discussing the whereabouts of Pincot.

-"Was it possible that he might have been studying till very late at night and slept somewhere in an isolated corner?"

She decided to go and check the entire Bungalow herself.

The Bungalow is constructed within a square plot of land measuring seven acres. In the centre is the big hall or the main drawing room. On the north and the south of the hall are three rooms each, and two rooms on the west side. All the rooms have doors opening into the main hall. So anyone going to any of those eight rooms must pass through the hall. The eight rooms have another door on the back side which opens into the garden and small individual lawns. Each room has an attached toilet.

This was the layout of the Bungalow which its former owner, the French businessman Mr. Pierre had made. When this came into the ownership of Mr. William Kutt, Annie's father, he extended the Bungalow by adding four wings of three rooms each on the four corners. Each wing is self-contained with attached bathrooms.

The main hall, along with the eight rooms opening into it, has now been converted into guest rooms. At least two dozen guests can be accommodated with all the amenities at any given time. Out of the four wings at the four corners, one is used by Annie's father, who lives alone after his wife's death, one wing is used by her brother Peterson, one wing by Annie herself and one wing is vacant at present. There are passages constructed for going from one wing to another. The passages, three feet wide, are covered with special Ranigunj tiles as is the entire high roof of the Bungalow, visible from as far as three miles away.

The Frenchman had constructed the Bungalow with a very high ceiling. The four wings added later have slightly lower heights and the passages further lower.

Annie began searching each wing. First, she entered the one used by Peterson. The first room had a clean made up bed, the second had every article neatly stacked and the third had an empty sofa which had been freshly dusted. Pincot was nowhere.

She then went to her father's wing. Here again, the first room had a cleanly made-up bed, and the second had clothes and other articles properly stacked. In the third room, there were two locked cupboards, while the third one was wide open. The sofa set was also clean and dusted. A lot of old papers, registers and files etc. were scattered on the carpet, with her father closely looking at each one of the deeds by taking it close to his eyes. The orderly Ramy Jamadar was standing by the side of the open cupboard.

"Rampur file", asked William and Ramy began looking for it in the cupboard. He quickly found it as if he knew the exact location and handed it over to his Master. Ramy has also grown old now.

Ramy Jamadar has been with his father since he was a young man. It is said that he was the first and the only person in this Dharampur village who went to meet William Kutt and stood by his side as his assistant when the Englishman had first arrived from Purnia with seven bullock carts loaded with luggage, tents and other essentials and having in possession a deed for one hundred acres of land allotted by the Collector of Purnia.

He had set up the camp in several tents in the eastern part of the village within wide open fields, just in front of the Frenchman's Bungalow. The entire village was rife with the news that a bunch of English Sahibs had descended on the village. People would come out of their houses, get a glimpse of the Sahibs from a distance and return to their house. They were afraid of these Sahibs. The party also had two red-turbaned sepoys for their protection. The red-turbaned sepoys were a terror in the villages those days.

When the sepoys looked at them, the villagers would run away till they were completely out of sight, safe and within the boundaries of their own courtyards. The womenfolk kept the children inside.

Ramy Jamadar tells lots of stories of that first day of their arrival, how he gathered courage and went to meet the Sahibs at the camp. He could gather the courage since his family had been mixing with the Sahibs for a long time, from the last generation. Long ago, in 1856, his father was one of the men in the army of the Governor-General Lord Dalhousie. His father had travelled to China, taken part in the Chinese war, had seen the Manchu Queen Xiaozheyi, he had also taken part in the Turkish war. He had retired after a long and distinguished service to the British. Ramy had been appointed to the same post after his father had retired. Although he was an ordinary sepoy, he boasted among the villagers that he was a Jamadar (an assistant sub-inspector). Since then he became famous as Ramy Jamadar within the locality around Dharamapur village. He served the British during the First World War. In that war, he lost one of his hands and he was discharged from service. Having served the British for two generations, Ramy was not afraid of the Sahibs. And he had walked to the camp fearlessly that day.

He had been surprised to find the head Sahib. Look, this is our Billi Kutta Sahib (a distortion of William Kutt's name, to suit the local dialect)! Needlessly the villagers got afraid of him. He used to tell Annie, "Do you know Ma'am?"

-"What?" Annie would ask eagerly.

-"Our country is a country of fools. People cannot pronounce the names of the British properly. So in the beginning William Kutt was called Billi Kutta (meaning cat dog) Sahib when he had set up his cotton trading business here in this village. And do you know?"

-"What?"

-"The Frenchman Mr. Pierre was responsible for spreading this distorted name."

-"Is that so?"

-"Yes, agreed that our people had difficulty in pronouncing British names correctly but at least Mr. Pierre could have done that. Instead, he also began callingWilliam Saheb Billi Kutta. Your father had quarrelled with him. He came from France, long before your father arrived here. He used to bring sacks of gold, give them to Jilebi Sahu (the local merchant) and take back bundles of fine cloth.

Our Sahib, your father, took first Jilebi Sahu into confidence and to his side. Then he drove Pierre away. It was not smooth work, however. I am telling you of the time before your birth. He fought with several local merchants and landlords. He eliminated Haji Hazrat Zafar Ali, the landlord Nawab who was very influential in this locality. Our Sahib grabbed the entire holding of that Nawab. Then Raja Samman Singh, Dewan Nirdhan Singh. One by one he went on grabbing their lands and driving them away from this locality. That is how he could accumulate so much land. He forcibly occupied this Bungalow immediately after the departure of Mr. Pierre. Then he constructed the four wings on the four corners. Lots of stories related to the acquisition of the property.

On the first day – a memorable day, the camp was being set up. Workers had come all the way from Purnia. They were erecting the tents. The sepoys sent by the Collector of Purnia were on the guard. I approached closer. Our Sahib noticed me and called, "Hey man."

I went straight and saluted him, "Yes Sir".

-"Are you from this village?" William Sahib had asked me.

-"Yes Sir."

-"What happened to your left hand?"

-"Yes Sir, it was amputated after the War, the First World War."

-"So you have served the British?"

-"Yes Sir."

-"Fine, can you bring three servants tomorrow?"

-"Yes Sir."

-"Will you also come?"

-"Sure Sir, I shall also be there."

-"Would you like to work?"

-"Of course Sir, I shall be happy."

-"Can you go to the shop now?"

-"Sure Sir, I shall go."

-...And you know Ma'am, I began working for your father from that very day. William Sahib was very fond of me. I became his confidant. So many things have happened since then - so many quarrels, so many agreements and reconciliations, and what not...."

Finding her father engrossed in work Annie returned back. Pincot was not there either.

She appeared on the veranda of the main drawing room where in front under a large sun umbrella were seated other members of the party on cane chairs. The cook Hamid, bearer Dinu, orderly Jamil and Siraj and the peons Bhola and Ramphal were standing close by in attendance.

There was a table in the centre on which were kept the morning breakfast, whisky bottle and glasses. One chair was kept vacant for Annie.

She went and sat down on the empty chair and straightway asked, "Any lead about Pincot?"

-"We didn't even give it a thought. We had been waiting for you. In fact I have already started with a few drinks. Hope you don't mind", said Jennie apologetically.

-"This is not the time for me to take offence. Let me know when each one of you got up and looked for Pincot and did not find him."

-"I got up around eight A.M." Pit recounted, "I did not find any sign of anyone else having woken up till that time. I came to the drawing room. All the rooms were bolted from the inside except Pincot's room which had its doors open."

-"Pincot's room was open?" Mary quickly questioned him.

-"Mary, it is not considered advisable to show more than necessary concern. I know you loved Pincot very much", Jennie interrupted her and finished her last drink.

-"How about Pincot?" Annie again inquired.

-"Pincot was not there. I thought he might be in the bathroom. But I did not find his blanket on his bed either which he often used to wrap around. I did not give it much thought and went to finish my morning chores."

-"Then when did you finally notice him missing?" Annie was getting impatient.

Tony replied, "I noticed that. My stuff was kept along with that of Pincot in the same bag, which belonged to him. The bag also contained my razor. You know I go to the bathroom only after shaving. I went to look for the razor. I was surprised to find neither the bag nor Pincot. But my razor had been kept on the table in the room. This alarmed me. I went around and told everyone about Pincot missing. We all went around looking for him but didn't find him."

-"When in the night was he seen last?" Annie probed the matter.

-"Around ten, when he returned after dinner with you. We had been taking our dinner in the main drawing room. He stood there for a brief while watching us, and then went back to his room. There was probably a book in his hand", Peterson added calmly.

-"Not probably, certainly he had a book in his hand."

-"Everyone had noticed the change in his behaviour for the last few days but beginning the evening of 31st December, the change had become alarming. He was altogether a transformed person", said Tony.

-"He had become very grave suddenly and would speak very little."

-"Where did he go after all?"

-"That's the question."

-"Did you ask the servants? Maybe someone saw him."

-"We did, no one saw him going or leaving any room."

-"Did you ask the security person at the main gate?"

-"Yes we did. He said that around a couple of hours before sunrise he went to the gate and asked the guard to open. The guard obeyed."

-"Did he say anything to the guard?"

-"No, nothing."

-"Really mysterious. Fine, please continue with your breakfast. I am just going to school for a while and shall be back soon." As she began walking the hall. Peterson followed her.

-"Is it so important?"

-"Yes, I have to go."

-"It would have been better if you stayed here."

-"Why?" Annie just stopped.

-"There is a chance of some violence."

-"What type of violence?"

-"Nothing serious, I shall handle it."

-"Tell me exactly what do you foresee."

-"Some farmers are refusing to cultivate indigo."

-"Why?"

-"They say there is no profit in indigo. Better they grow foodgrains."

-"They are right."

-"No, they are not right. Fine, try to come back soon."

By that time they reached the portico. While climbing the stairs, Annie asked, "Where is Jennie?"

-"In number one."

-"Are you okay?"

-"I took just a single drink."

-"I implore you to not venture towards the field in this state."

Peterson turned back. But he did not go back to the lawn, he went to his own wing. Orderly Jameel and the peon Ramphal saw him. They ran towards him and stopped at the gate.

- "Jameel".

-"Yes Sir"

-"Get three guns and clean them thoroughly. Where is Ramphal?"

-"Yes Sir"

And the two shuddered. From head to foot, they began trembling. Ramphal felt as if his throat was getting dry very fast. His feet were just not moving to go into the room to get the guns.

Today he got up sneezing, it was a bad omen and then his path was intercepted by a cat, another bad omen. He had become afraid that time. Now hearing about cleaning guns, he became terrified.

He knew today the indigo farmers would oppose Peterson's plan. They would no longer cultivate indigo.

The old man William too got angry on many occasions, but it was nothing like his son Peterson. He would use divisive tricks to crush the rebellion. A clever move. No bloodshed.

That is how he could drive away Mr. Pierre. With only such clever moves he could bring Jilebi Sahu and the entire Jolaha clan to his side. His clever tricks dislodged Raja Samman Singh and Nawab Haji Hazrat Zafar Ali. There was hardly any bloodshed, except once in the beginning when he had to open fire at three persons belonging to Mr. Pierre. And then some firing during that year's wartime. That's all. But Peterson...!

Ramphal recalled the last incident. Peterson killed three persons with just one gun, came back, sat and began drinking non-stop that continued the whole night.

-"Ramphal?" Peterson called.

-"Yes Sir", Ramphal ran towards the room.

-"Where is Bhola?"

-"He is in the lawn, Sir." And he ran to call Bhola.

-"Jameel?" Another call.

-"Yes Sir." Jameel appeared before his Master.

-"Clean his gun as well. I am sending him."

-"Yes Sir."

By that time Bhola had arrived, trembling.

-"Ramdhan, Sirichan and Ramphal would go to the fields among the farmers. They would call all the farmers engaged in indigo farming in the northern part of the village. Exactly at three in the afternoon."

-"Yes Sir."

-"What time?"

-"Exactly at three in the afternoon, Sir." Bhola saluted the Master and ran away.

Peterson looked at some papers for a minute and then called, "Ramphal"

-"Yes Sir."

-"Munshi (the accountant) Mr. Giridhari Das, Manager Mr. Sanyal, Assistant Manager Mr. Singh, and the Gumasta (Estate agent, also clerk) Badri!"

Ramphal turned back to call all of them.

Jameel was cleaning the guns. He quickened the pace of work.

-"Peterson", Tony came there.

-"Tony! How are you here?"

-"What are you up to?" Tony poured two glasses of drinks and gave one to Peterson.

Peterson replied, "I was just looking for some papers."

-"No, objectionable. We are here. No work for your Estate. We feel humiliated."

-"But why?"

-"Because we are sitting all alone."

Peterson sipped once and said, "You all and alone? Who all are there?"

-"There is no host on the table. Neither Annie nor you. We need your permission."

-"Permission? For what?"

-"We want to leave immediately."

-"What? But it's not even a week. You were supposed to stay much longer."

-"All our programmes are upset. Pincot has upset them. Come with me quickly and bring another bottle."

-"What? There are no bottles there. Sirichan? Ramdhan? Dinu? Where are these people gone?"

-"Yes Sir, I shall go and call them immediately." Jameel left the guns and ran.

Annie stopped for a second near Maria's room and then entered.

-"Please come in", Maria was leaning against the wall on the bed with her gze fixed on the wall. There was a half-empty glass lying in front of her and a cigarette in hand, smoke spreading out of that all around.

-"What have you been thinking?" Annie asked sitting on the bed.

-"Not able to think anything clearly. Just sitting and troubling you all."

-"It seems you were disturbed..."

-"What?"

-"You know well, that Mary is dull and jealous."

-"Annie", Maria finished the glass in one gulp, took a long puff and spoke, "To tell you the truth, I was not teasing her, but rather teasing myself."

-"What's that?" Annie appeared surprized.

-"You had asked who saw him last. To tell you the truth, it was me, I had seen him at eleven-thirty."

-"Eleven-thirty?"

-"Yes, and was with him till one in the morning."

-"Had he called you?"

-"No."

-"No! Then?"

-"I went to his room myself."

-"Yourself?"

Maria did not utter a word. She just kept looking at the cigarette trapped between her fingers.

-"What are you thinking?"

-"Nothing."

-"I don't agree. You are certainly thinking about something but you don't want to tell."

-"You had asked but I could not tell you. Now, that incident has become very important in my life."

-"What?", Annie looked straight at Maria.

-"Annie, will you tell everything without any hesitation?" Maria asked.

-"I normally do not try to speak lies."

-"That I know, everyone knows. That's why I am asking."

-"Go ahead."

-"Okay, did anything special happen on the evening of the 31st December?"

-"Nothing special."

-"Sure?"

-"Absolutely sure."

-"He went straight to your room after coming here that day. Right? And if my recollection is not wrong, he returned only after eleven-thirty in the night."

-"Yes, your recollection is correct."

-"So nothing happened in between?"

-"Believe me, nothing."

-"Didn't he try?"

-"There was a storm of lust rising but against the firmness of Alps, the storm dissipated."

-"Didn't he try again after that?"

-"No."

-"Surprising."

-"Yes, because there was not only stone firmness in the Alps, there was absolutely no encouragement of greenery at all."

-"But he was drunk and I know you hate liquor. Even so?"

-"Men can become wild in lust."

-"Possible, but you have to consider my responses as well."

-"What response? Can one overcome Nature?"

-"Sure. No doubt Nature is very powerful but not beyond control."

-"In this journey of conquering, you must be struggling." Maria observed.

-"That I cannot say exactly. It's possible sometimes for brief moments I might be struggling but certainly, that's momentary, fleetingly small and insignificant. The second point is that my engagements are such that even that fleeting moment hardly gets a chance to arise and shake me up. It changes direction. ... But why are you asking me these questions?"

-"I am surprised."

-"About what?"

-"Questions have been arising in my mind what after all is the reason for Pincot's attraction towards you."

-"Did you find any reason?" Annie asked.

-"A simple reason."

-"What?"

-"The attraction of the unreachable, like one is attracted to Mount Everest. Actually, this is human nature, seen mainly among men. Men are basically stubborn and aggressive. They try to show that they are unbeatable. They don't want to let anything go... Am I correct?"

-"If not totally, you are certainly quite close to the truth. And the other?"

-"The other is your personality, its elitist and noble features, its dignity, the hidden decency, the beauty."

-"Oh, that's all about your vocabulary of the adjectives."

-"But Annie, if truth be told, even with all the words of praise, probably it still wouldn't suffice to describe the inner radiance of your character. To do this, I must turn myself into a man."

-"Go ahead, become a man and then look into me." And Annie lovingly pulled Maria's cheeks.

-"Ha Ha! A man has gone missing trying to look into you. God knows where he is and how much will he suffer. And then you suggest me to become a man! If at all I do, I will not come anywhere near you."

-"Why?" Annie laughed loudly.

-"You possess beauty but not emotion, you are pretty but not warm. You have a balanced development of physique but not passion, which attracts men to a woman."

-"That you have to find out by becoming a man", Annie smiled.

-"That is impossible and that's why I am jealous."

-"Jealous of me?"

-"Yes."

-"Why?"

-"Because you changed Pincot according to your wishes. The poor chap adopted all your manners. He even began wrapping your blanket around him all the while. Most likely he has carried it away as a souvenir. Your style of eating, your manners of sitting, your philosophy, he copied them all. As a woman, what more can one desire to win a man? Total submission. That's why I am jealous."

-"Maria", Annie turned serious, "This is certainly not a mean achievement, but rather a very uncommon and great one. It's a social transformation. This is not a matter of jealousy but of pride for us all."

-"But Annie, how did this sudden transformation take place?"

-"It wasn't as sudden as you may think. Its seeds had been shown some two years ago. It was growing slowly, but it only needed a push at the opportune moment and that arrived when he came to my room on that year-end evening."

-"What type of push?"

-"First, as I explained, the rock-like opposition to his lust, my complete neglect, snub and just at that moment his remembering his dead mother. You know he loved his mother very much. Lately, he had been thinking of her too much."

-"Really?"

-"He had been told that his mother was a member of a German spy ring and she had been killed in a road accident. He was very sad about that. His mother came again to his recollection that evening we met."

-"So these were the circumstances that set him to undergo the transformation, is that so?"

-"Possible."

-"And from that moment I began experiencing a special attraction towards him. Magnetic, a greed of enormous proportion. I shall narrate my experience of last night later. First, one more question to you."

-"What?"

-"When he was completely transformed and he became totally agreeable to you, what were your feelings? Any greed?" Maria lighted the cigarette. Annie kept quiet for a while and did not tell anything. She began looking at Maria's face.

Looking at Maria, her adorable and beautiful face and body, made further shapely by the touch of men. Her lips held the burning cigarette, a serpentine thin line of smoke billowing out of the cigarette, moving upwards.

Her question "Any greed?" began whirling in her mind.

What? When? She recalled the incident of her holding Pincot's hand. Why did she do so?

The night of 31st December. Sitting on a mat of folded blanket to eat his dinner in Indian style. Facing each other.

Rice on the large plate, Dal in a bowl, and vegetables on various small plates. But he could not mix rice and dal properly as Indians do. There was no spoon, no fork or knife, as Annie does not normally use them. He would try but would not succeed. Roopy began laughing. She could have helped him mix rice and dal and also help him take the morsel into his mouth, but Annie did not allow that. Instead she herself held Pincot's hand and began guiding him.

-"Why don't you say something, Annie?" Maria was impatient as she had probed an inner quarter of the personality.

-"I am looking for the answer; nothing concrete is coming to mind."

Maria observed Annie's grave look and vacant eyes. She threw the cigarette and held Annie's face in both her hands.

-"Will you mind joining me for a drink?"

-"No, thanks."

-"Why?"

-"It does not suit my way of life."

-"What is your way of life?"

-"My way of life is the Indian philosophy which abolishes darkness."

-"Is it really so simple?"

-"Forget it. Tell me your experience of last night, which you volunteered but stopped."

-"I told you that I began to feel an unfathomable attraction towards him after his transformation. My urge to get him became very strong. You know that my urge to get any man has been so dominant that I have not cared of the consequences but always won. I have always felt men to be easy prey. But Pincot turned out to be different. The more I felt attracted towards him the more difficult it became to reach him. The main difficulty was your presence – he was almost always with you. Even last evening he was with you till dinner time. Probably both of you had gone somewhere in the early evening hours. All this hindrance in approaching him led to my jealousy. I became adamant – I had to win over him whatever the cost."

Maria stopped to light a cigarette again. Annie kept looking at her face throughout. She understood the words came from deep within Maria's soul. A true depiction of an infatuated woman. Maria continued, "In the night when everyone went to bed, I went to his room. He was reading a book. He looked at me and with a cold expression in his eyes, told me to sit down. There was no warmth or cordiality in his words unlike on previous occasions. I felt humiliated, became irritated and I became ever more determined to win over him.

I turned back and closed the door. Took the second blanket lying on the bed and wrapped it around myself. I snatched the book from his hand, threw it on the floor and sat very close to him, touching him. We were so close that our breaths were getting mixed. He moved backwards a little, I followed and moved close to him again...

-"Is it the smell that bothers you?" I asked.

-"Of course, but not to that extent." Pincot replied.

-"Should I make a drink for you?"

-"No, I have given up drinking beginning the New Year's Eve."

-"Forever?"

-"Shall try."

-"Will you not accede to my request?"

-"Please forgive me."

-"Did you give it up on the orders of Annie?"

-"No, voluntarily."

-"Why?"

-"Can't say exactly."

-"Is it to get closer to Annie?"

-"No one can get close to her."

-"Why?"

-"She is out of the reach of the ordinary, Very high."

-"Are you trying to reach her by wrapping this blanket around, becoming vegetarian, giving up drinking?"

-"These are not the preparations. These are not for Annie alone. But if I did manage to become even a fraction of what she has achieved, I shall consider myself fortunate. That will be a matter of great pride."

I got further irritated. I extinguished the lamp by extending my hand. Now the room was pitch dark. The darkness swallowed his unblemished and indifferent face as well.

He sat just like that, inactive and peaceful. Completely devoid of any emotion, any action. I was overcome by a desire to have him and quickly. I was trembling with emotion. My lust was at its peak. I was so excited that even my throat went dry. My heartbeat increased and breathing became abnormal.

I held him and put my mouth on his, began licking it violently, kissing would have been too mild an action. I held him tightly in my arms and rubbed my bare body against his. Finally, he was aroused and came to action."

Maria became silent for a moment and took a deep puff. Lowering her face as if hiding, she continued, "Annie, true that I won but that was worse than a defeat. Although I satisfied myself at that moment, it was much more painful than the unsatisfied state. In reality, I came to realise how poor have I become by demanding something. How poor a woman is? I now hated myself.

... But I also got to know his greatness. Possibly he understood my motives. He must have guessed the meaning of my subsequent inaction and idleness. He began caressing me, his fingers moving slowly in my hair. None of us would speak anything, as if the words had become shy. How and when I fell asleep I have no recollection. When I woke up I did not find him on the bed. It was difficult to find anything in such darkness. I thought he might have gone to the bathroom.

I came out and slept in my own room. I got up very late, much later than others. By that time everyone had found out that he had vanished. Telling you the truth, I was stunned. Now there is no scope to even ask for forgiveness. That will keep me hurting all my life. He is great, it's true.

... Even though this incident has not much significance for me, I have always fulfilled all my ambitions. I never waited for my fortune to assist me. But my begging last night demonstrates my poverty. I am very poor, very mean."

-"Maria, do not get carried away by an inferiority complex. You are great."

-"Great? Me? What are you saying? Such a mean person as I?"

-"You were, but no longer."

Maria looked at Annie with great astonishment and pity. Transient surprise, however, vanished quickly. She asked, "How?"

-"You have become great by your most recent experience. Such an experience is a treasure for a human being. You should cherish it. You will consider this incident an accomplishment of your life."

Maria felt overwhelmed. She replied, "Annie, you are really great."

She placed her head in Annie's lap and held her tightly in her arms. Annie began caressing Maria's back. She felt as if Maria was weeping.

Both remained in that condition for quite a while. Annie finally lifted Maria's head, wiped her tears and said, "Do you know one important aspect of Indians?"

-"What?" She looked at Annie's face.

-"Indians believe that if one ever takes a bath in the river Ganga even once, all the sins of the last seven births are washed away. Total sublimation."

-"Is that so? Do you believe in their concept of rebirth?"

-"Do you believe in the concept of inherited characters?"

-"What?"

-"I mean hereditary traits. Psychologists agree to only two aspects of character building – one is hereditary and the other is environment. And this is scientific. If the hereditary concept is true and scientific then equally so is rebirth."

-"Annie, we shall discuss these later in detail. I am stuck at some points and may be because you have left a couple of these untouched. But again I am getting jealous of you."

-"Again, why?" Annie smiled.

-"This jealousy came to me two days ago also and today again, but the two are for very different reasons. I repent why this jealousy did not come earlier."

-"You are getting wrong. The first was really jealousy, the second one was not. Besides everything has a destined time. How you feel today could not have come earlier, the time was just not ripe. The time came now and it came to you without delay."

-"Where did you learn all this?"

-"My mother came from Dr. Grierson's family, she was my first teacher, then with some reading and finally from a Guru here."

-"Who is your Guru here? Manik?"

-"No, Manik's father."

-"What is special about him?"

-"It is less to be described, more to be experienced."

-"Wah! Then you are lucky that you got the Guru and the disciple at the same place."

For some time both Maria and Annie kept quiet. Then Annie got up and left.

*

When Annie started for school, it was noon on the drawing room clock. She came to the gate. The Gorkha watchman saluted her and opened the gate.

-"Sher Bahadur?"

-"Yes Ma'am."

-"When did Pincot come out in the morning?"

-"Almost an hour before Sunrise."

-"But that was not the time for you to open the gate."

-"Surely not for everyone, Ma'am."

-"Did he tell anything?"

-"Nothing. He came here, and I opened the gate."

-"In which direction did he go?"

-"I could see him up to the Bazaar. He couldn't be seen beyond."

Annie moved forward.

After the gate, there are two roads. One goes along the boundary wall of the Bungalow, just wide enough for one bullock cart to pass, the unpaved mud road. The stable for the horses and the cattle shed are situated along this road, behind which is the large courtyard and the godown (warehouse) number three. Jute bales are stored here. The number one and number two godowns are situated behind the Bungalow at the far end. The entire Bungalow campus is surrounded by five-foot-high walls on the three sides.

Just in front of the gate is a much wider road paved with bricks, which runs up to half a furlong; then this merges into a mud road. On the two sides of the paved portion of the road, there are several small rooms. The inner gates of these rooms made of mud bricks and tin roofs with small verandas open into a courtyard. The tin roofs are somewhat higher. Enough use of wood in these rooms.

Servants of various grades, peons, cooks, bearers, orderlies, and the like occupy these rooms on the left. On the right side lives Manager Mr. P. Sanyal. He occupies three such rooms. The two rooms are used by his family and the third is his office.

The fourth room is allocated to Assistant Manager Ramaudar Singh for his office. Mr. Singh belongs to this village and he does not need rooms for his family. The next rooms, one each, are allocated to Badri Gumasta, to accountant Giridhari Das, to Ramphal, and to the three Gorkha watchmen.

Even though many people are from this village, they are required to stay within the campus and they are on duty all the time. That is the reason they have been allocated rooms here.

All these arrangements have been made by Mr. William himself. During those days, when he had driven Mr. Pierre away, and grabbed this Bungalow along with all the land, he had constructed these hutments. He managed to grab the land belonging to Haji Hazrat Zafar Ali and expanded his Estate and the Bungalow. Then he added the lands belonging to Raja Samman Singh and Dewan Nirdhan Singh as well.

His retinue of servants also grew accordingly at each stage.

On both sides of the paved portion of the road, after the servants' quarters, there are about two dozen shops. Most of them are for groceries, a few for clothes, a few also for sundry cheap imitation jewellery, some sweetmeat shops, also with items like *Chiura* (flattened rice) and curd, which locals relish for breakfast, and then a few tea stalls, a couple of *pan* (betel leaf/nut) shops and also a few tailors' shops.

All these shops form part of what is known as Kothi[2] Bazaar. Such a bazaar was the idea of Mr. William himself. He just constructed the rooms and traders of various hues began approaching for setting up shops. Some came from the village market and some others also from distant places. There was only one condition imposed by Mr. William: the shop must be good and also must sell goods a little cheaper than what is available in the village markets around.

But one needed an application to be written and submitted. That was done by Badri Gumasta. He is surrounded by people intending to submit an application.

-"Do you have the requisite capital to run the shop?" asks Badri Gumasta.

-"Yes Sir, I have."

-"The shop should be good, not just a tottering one"

-"Shall try to make it very good, Sir."

-"Do you know the rent?"

-"Yes Sir, I know."

-"How much?"

-"Two rupees, Sir."

-"Do you know you will have to sell items at a price little lower than the village market."

-"No problem Sir."

-"Have you brought my *dasturi*[3]?"

-"How much, Sir?"

-"You don't know?" Badri Gumasta would stop writing and keep the pen on his ear. Now he would not write the application for that person. And Mr. William approves the applications

---

[2] *Kothi :* a colloquial name for the Bungalow or a large residential complex belonging to the rich.

[3] *Dasturi :* payment made for a service, a kind of tip.

written only by Badri Gumasta. Only when William Sahib approves, the shop will be allotted.

Shopkeepers are rushing to try their luck. They know where the future lies. The shops in the village market are closing and those in the Kothi Bazaar are bustling.

The shop selling clothes is the hot pick because Mr. William has himself brought three Marwaris from Calcutta. Those three shops are overflowing with a large variety of very colourful and fashionable saris, dhotis, Shantipuri, Nayansukh brands, Aam Chhap, *gamchha* (a kind of towel used by village folk), *ganji* (vests) etc. procured directly from England.

One can purchase the clothes and then give them to the tailor then and there. No need to run around. Three tailors sitting in a row, very busy, with not even a minute to spare for leisure.

There is no leisure for even the tea shop owner. One tea shop owner has been brought by Mr. William from Calcutta. Five cups of tea for a *paisa* (sixty-four paise made a Rupee then). Adjacent to the tea shop is the *pan* shop.

The trader dealing in pots and pans has come from Forbesgunj. *Tharis* (a kind of large plate made of brass, German Silver or similar alloys), bowls, *lotas* (water pots), ladles, frying pans, large and small utensils and other kitchen utilities decorated attractively on the shelves in rows are all available here.

All the shops are always crowded with customers. People from faraway places come to Kothi Bazaar, buy goods, and enjoy tea and *pan*. The tea shop owner left for Calcutta but he taught five locals the art of making good tea. People come to the Bazaar from as far away as seven-eight miles, just to have a cup of tea. Just throw one *paisa* and get five people to have tea together. What is special about it? Just take a cup of tea and the headache is gone, cough vanishes, fever disappears.

Earlier there used to be some seven-eight grocery shops in the centre of the village at the *chauraha*. There were no cloth shops, no tailor and no tea shops at all. Only one shop for the handlookm clothes from the local weavers. Dull and coarse, nothing like the fancy clothes from England. No one even peeps through these shops anymore.

People run to Kothi Bazaar. Varieties of fancy clothes, colourful, plaids and patterns, and soft, and cheaper too. The entire locality is buzzing with the appreciation of such goods.

People bring paddy in sacks, and shawls, carrying on their heads, some also bring rice, jute etc. There are some eight-to-ten middlemen, who buy those goods. Get cash and buy whatever you want in the Bazaar.

Rich people bring their goods on bullock carts, sell to the middlemen and then go to the clothes shop, utensil shop....

Shops are as yet in the process of beig set up. There are twenty-two rooms to be let out as yet. And people from around the locality are running to rent shops. They are running to get the application written by Badri Gumasta. Some even try to influence him through various means. They know that only when the application is written by Badri Gumasta that Mr. William will at all consider it. Then only there can be a chance to get the shop allotted which is a sure way to rake in profits and mint money.

The traders of the locality are desperate. Badri Gumasta's behavior increases this desperation. Everyone knows that there are only twenty-two shops to let out. This is the order of William Sahib.

People are running. They bring ghee, fish, curd, rice, *gur* for Badri Gumasta. Very few have cash to spare but they can offer *dasturi* in kind. Sacks full of rice are being sent to Badri Gumasta.

But Badri Gumasta does not take his pen down from his ear. He is quietly weighing those *dasturies* from various traders. He does not write more than two applications in a day. On being prodded, he gets angry and shouts, "Do you think getting a shop in Kothi Bazaar is so cheap? Go and first find out and then come back."

-"I have come from a faraway place, Sir. No one knew the *dasturi* there", someone pleads.

-"Are you speaking the truth?"

-"Yes Sir."

-"Will any respectable person of this village agree to stand guarantee for you?"

-"I can manage, Sir."

-"Then listen, for you, it will be Fifteen Rupees, one sack of rice, one container of ghee. If you agree to this then come back tomorrow or the day after as per your convenience."

He looks at another person standing nearby.

-"What's the matter with you?"

-"The same issue Sir."

Badri recognises the person.

-"Yes I have already received the *dasturi* you sent. Sit down."

Badri Gumasta takes the pen from his ear and begins writing the application.

All these are the tales of the time when Kothi Bazaar was being set up. ....

Annie does not go to the school via Kothi Bazaar. She prefers the mud road along the boundary wall. In the stable horses are busy eating. The horsemen see her coming. They become conscious and salute her. Next comes the cattle shed. Cattle herders are feeding the cattle while ploughmen are working on hay to turn it into readymade fodder. On one side of the cattle shed a number of *sampani*[4] carts are lined up. The carriage-men are cleaning the carriages.

All these people line up to pay respect to Annie. Everyone is surprised that Ma'am is so late for school.

-"Jeetan"

-"Yes Ma'am", The cart driver Jeetan responds with alarm.

-"Is *sampani* in order?"

-"Yes Ma'am, cleaned and ready."

-"I may use it in the evening."

-"Sure Ma'am", Jeetan again salutes her.

Annie moves on. After the cattle shed, is the big courtyard, with piles after piles of paddy and hay, with heaps and heaps of hay scattered around. Kothidar Ramphal is there to oversee paddy getting threshed. A number of oxen tethered on a single rope tied to the central bamboo pole go round and round on a huge bed of paddy spread around on the ground. Numerous bundles of harvested paddy remain stacked over a large area at other places in the compound.

The school is situated on the northwest corner of the Bungalow, almost on the edge of the village. There is a mango orchard in between, covering an area of some ten to twelve acres. Had there been no orchard, the school would have been visible from this spot on the boundary of the Bungalow.

Annie traverses this distance every day on foot. She does it of her own will. Although there is a separate *sampani* cart for her use, there is the cart driver, but she does not use it. There is also a separate palanquin for her use with four bearers. Both the cart and the palanquin are ready all the time, twenty-four hours, for her use.

---

[4] *Sampani:* A type of fully covered carriage, made of wood and drawn by bullocks, used to carry women of noble families.

All the servants have got land from the Estate. There is no tax on that land. You just grow whatever you want and eat. But be ready with the cart and the palanquin all the time.

William Sahib had his own *sampani* cart, two palanquins – one fully covered and another partially covered. That *sampani* cart is now old and broken, no longer in use.

Annie's *sampani* cart is brand new; this was made by a special carpenter brought from Calcutta. In the earlier cart, the roof was made of wood only. In the new one, the wood is covered with tin on top. There is no chance of it leaking during the rains. There are small windows on all sides with pieces of tarpaulin hanging which can be lifted and tied if one wants to. There are cushioned seats on both sides along the length of the cart. Four persons can comfortably sit inside it.

Annie and Pincot had used this cart to go to the *Chamar* (shoemakers) Tola yesterday. The cart driver Jeetan had been requesting Annie for the last several days to make a visit to the *Chamar* Tola. It was since the Christian shoemakers had beaten Jeetan's mother, belonging to the Hindu *Chamar* Tola, on the pretext of calling her a witch. In the Christian *Chamar* Tola, Dukhi Chamar's son Johan's wife is sick. Whatever medicines she tries doesn't help. She has even taken recourse to faith healers and sorcerers but of no help. She remains ill and possessed by a ghost. Everyone there doubts that it is Jeetan's mother's tricks. People have always suspected that she is a witch.

Jeetan knows his mother is innocent. And this is the reason for the tension between the two religious groups.

The *Chamar* Tola is situated on the southern edge of the village. Although it is called *Chamar* Tola, there are some *Dusadh* families also living within the hamlet. As their number is small, the colony is referred to as the *Chamar* Tola because of them being in the majority.

Earlier there was only one *Chamar* Tola. On the west of this Tola some distance away is the cluster of houses where some twenty-five *Musahar* families live. This is called *Musahari*. Further south and west, leaving some three-four acres of land in between, is the cluster of houses belonging to the vegetable growers and Muslims.

These two clusters, *Musahari* and Muslim Tola, fall within the jurisdiction of Bhagalpur District as per land survey records. But for all practical purposes, they are part of Dharampur village. This part of the village is known for *Chamars* and Muslims. *Musahars* are not counted at all.

This hamlet became famous when a pastor came here. In the very beginning when William Kutt had arrived with tents and carts, a couple of white people came along too. Among them was a pastor.

The pastor used to roam around this part of the village, lecturing people, and trying to brainwash them. He would distribute small lemon candies to the children. The children called him Padi (a distortion of Padri for the pastor) Sahib.

The Padri Sahib persuaded the Collector of Bhagalpur and got some land allocated here. He constructed a small thatched school a little distance away in the south. He also constructed a big thatched house and called it the Church. He installed a big bell in the church.

He was helped generously by the Collectors of Purnia and Bhagalpur in his mission. Later William Sahib also helped him. He would donate sacks of rice and other provisions to the church.

Padri Sahib would distribute the provisions among the *Chamartoli* (*Chamar*'s Tola), *Dusadhatoli* (Dusadh's Tola), Musalman Tola, *Musahari* and also among the vegetable growers. These people were generally poor. They would be obliged and praise him.

They would praise him because he also used to treat people with illnesses. The Padri Sahib had a box which contained some mixtures. A servant would carry the box wherever Padri Sahib would go. The medicine was fast-acting. One dose and the headache would be gone. Similarly, one dose was enough to treat the fever. One dose of another medicine could stop someone's dysentery.

Although Padri Sahib toured the entire village, he would spend more time in those parts where *Chamars, Musahars, Dusadhs*, and Muslims lived. But he would not spend more time with the Muslim landlord Haji Hazrat Zafar Ali, instead would be seen with poor Muslims. As Haji was the landlord, Muslim Tola was also referred to as Haji Tola.

When Haji's lands were grabbed by William Sahib, Padri Sahib stopped going anywhere. He would now spend time in that so-called church. He would teach in the church premises (called Padri's school), would treat people with illness, and distribute medicines to those who visited him. Depending on the needs of the poor, he would persuade William Sahib to give some rice also.

-" Oh, no food for the last two days?" Padri would ask. Long bearded heads would begin shaking in reply.

-"No food Sir".

-"Would you come to the church daily in the evening?"

-"Yes Sir, I shall surely come."

He would give a small change to someone, would write a slip and send it to William Sahib and so on.

-"What's wrong with you?" He would ask another person standing nearby.

-"Stomach pain, Sir."

-"Promise to come to the church in the evening?"

-"Promised Sir."

He would get a dose of medicine which would cure his ailment.

-"What about you?" He would ask the third.

-"Fever Sir, for the last seven days."

-"Come to the church in the evening?"

-"Yes Sir, without fail."

He would get his medicine and leave. Padri Sahib would close his eyes. On opening his eyes, he would surely find someone standing there in need of his help.

-"Yes?"

-"Sir, fever on alternate nights."

-"Would you come to the church in the evening?"

-"Yes Sir."

He would give medicine to that person too. Very few children would initially come to his school. But he was not worried.

Finally one day Padri Sahib left the village. When he left, many people became sad. Some had even wept.

Among those who wept were people from Christian *Chamartoli, Musahari* and Musalman Tola. Padri had done a lot of work for the villagers. He also quietly upset people and divided them. Not only he divided them, but he created a new caste and gave birth to a new society. A new Tola was settled, for those who had adopted Christianity following Padri's persuasion. Among *Chamars* about eighteen-twenty families had converted, they now belonged to the Christian *Chamartoli*. The conversion ceremony was held in the church. Prayers were held, and the bell rang loudly.

The new Christian Tola consisted of some Muslim families, a few *Musahar* families and a few *Dusadh* families. But there were problems too. Some families had not changed their names. Among *Musahars* no one had got jobs either. They had not accepted even water from Padri Sahib's hands. When Padri Sahib left and these families found themselves getting insulted by their own folks in addition to others among Christians, they returned to their native fold.

The old folks in *Musahari* sat together and discussed the issues. Finally, they agreed to condone the converted and took them back into their fold. People were happy that finally, they had saved their religion.

There was a loss of religion for those who remained in the Christian Tola. But several of them had got jobs. So they were not bothered. The orderlies and peons working in the Bungalow of William Sahib had been appointed only after converting to Christianity. Some people had been employed in the school. There had been plans to make a *pucca* building for the church. But suddenly Padri Sahib received a letter from Madras. He left the village immediately.

Soon the school became deserted. The boys began tending to cattle as usual. The womenfolk began pulling thatchings from the church and school's thatched roofs for fire. Men would pull the bamboo pieces supporting roof. Slowly both the school and the church were pulled down as there was no one to look after.

But Christianity survived. That stuck with some people. The Hindus and Muslims were adamant not to allow the converts back into their fold. The Thakurs and Brahmans were upset with these converts from the very beginning. They had been annoyed because the converts behaved arrogantly and thought as if they had won something big. They considered themselves a different society, placed above those of traditional Hindus and Muslims. Christianity gave them some training to wear clean clothes, many of them had jobs and had cash also in hand. Even those who had not got regular jobs, used to get seasonal employment for sundry work in the Kothi. The rule in Kothi was such that even for sundry jobs, those who had converted to Christianity were getting preferences over others in the village. During

Christmas, they had enjoyed a feast with Padri Saheb at the church.

Once they ate the feast, they considered themselves like the British, nothing less. Their temper would always run high.

But when Padri Sahib left, all the feasts and celebrations came to an end. Then the temper of those Christians also sobered, as if they came down to earth from high above the sky. Nevertheless, the society had been divided.

Even while leaving, the Padri taught them that they were superior to the common folk as they were the sons of Christ.

It was one of those sons of Christ, Johan, who had gone from the Christian *Chamartoli* and beat Jeetan's mother. Jeetan had been trying to request Annie Ma'am for the last several days to find time to go and have a *Panchayat* (meeting of village juries) to discuss and settle the issue.

Yesterday while going on her *sampani* cart with Pincot to *Chamartoli* for the *Panchayat*, she noticed Manik, as the windows of *sampani* were all open. He had been coming from the direction in which they were going.

"Hello Manik", Annie called him excitedly. She had not met him for the last week because the school had been closed due to Christmas. Manik had left for Prayag as per his earlier plans on the very day when the school closed was another reason.

Annie had been inquiring about his return just after four days of his departure. He had returned that day itself most likely. Annie was very happy. She had been very curious about Manik's return. She was done with knitting the sweater. As soon as the cart came closer, she shouted to Jeetan, "Hey, stop the cart." Looking from the window she said, "Good evening Manikji. Greetings for the New Year. When did you return?"

Manik was also excited. He replied, "Same to you, I returned today."

*

Annie's plan for a school had been rejected by the father-son duo. Neither William Sahib nor Peterson had liked the idea. When she had arrived from Calcutta and began talking to people here, she learnt that a young man named Manik Jha and another elderly gentleman called Mohan Mani, educated in Patna, were quite influential around the villages and also involved in both social work and the Independence Movement.

Annie had sent one of the Kothi's orderlies with a letter, inviting both Manik and Mohan Mani to come and convince her father and brother, stating, "I have a plan to start an English school in this village. I have been talking to my father and younger brother. But they do not approve the plan. I feel it will be a great service to the local society where children could study English along with other subjects. I have learnt that both of you are into social service. I am sure you will appreciate my plan. Please come tomorrow to discuss the school issue. It is very important." They had promised to help her.

That day Annie had been waiting in the lawn with her father and brother. Within a short while the gate opened and both Manik and Mohan Mani were seen entering the campus. She met both of them for the first time. Both were clad in dhoti, local traditional style. Mohan Mani, in his mid-forties, was suave, soft-spoken and grave-looking. Manik Jha, possibly in his late twenties or early thirties, was a handsome young man, very persuasive and vocal in his approach.

They sat down. Annie introduced herself. Talks and discussions were held over a tea session, and after that, both William Sahib and Peterson were convinced about the usefulness of an English medium school in the village.

Manik had said, "The plan of an English medium school has been started by you people, I mean the British only."

-"How?" William Sahib had asked. He was not connected with the world of education and had no interest in that either. Earlier he was hawking clothes, then he became a farmer, step-by-step a big farmer and then a small landlord, owner of the Bungalow, then a big landlord. He had traversed a very different route. That's why he was surprised to hear about the British initiative.

-"See, after 1772 the British rule in India began under East India Company. In 1781 Lord Warren Hastings himself started a Madarsa in Calcutta. After that in 1791, with the effort of British Resident Jonathan Duncan, Sanskrit College was started at Benaras (now Varanasi). Fort William College was established in 1800."

-"Surely with the British initiatives, education, especially modern education developed in India."

William Sahib was listening silently, captivated by such words. He did not like these two gentlemen. These two were the biggest enemies of his Estate and he would become helpless at times before them.

There was enough reason for his helplessness. These two controlled not only the people of this village, but most of the tenants of his Estate from other villages too. They are the leaders of all the tenants, peasants and labourers. On just one call from either of the two, the entire peasantry can assemble to a place. These two are also the leaders of the Self-Rule movement and the independence movement. They wield a lot of respect among the people in the locality.

Even William Sahib is in awe. He silently respects them and hence has kept quiet while they have been talking.

-"We shall certainly be grateful to you people. Not only that" – finding William Sahib attentive and grave and thinking he was making a positive impact, Manik added further in his zeal, "Governor General Lord Hastings himself had been in favour of

Western education in India and therefore he appointed his legal member Macaulay as the Chairman of the Education Committee. While declaring his education policy in 1835, Macaulay had laid stress on the propagation of English education among Indians."

-"Macaulay?"

-"Yes, Macaulay."

-"I have heard his name", William Sahib responded softly.

-"Based on that policy of Macaulay, Lieutenant Governor James Thompson, keeping in mind the local requirements, had advocated the propagation of education in every village and town. But maximum work in this direction was done by the Chairman of the Board of Control Charles Wood Sahib."

-"Chairman of the Board of Control?" William Sahib had been taken aback. The Board of Control is itself a very high-powered entity, and the Chairman of that Board worked to propagate English education in India! Oh, how much have the British done for this country! Who says that they came here only to plunder? Not only they have taken, but they have also given a lot.

William Sahib was woken from slumber. He began taking interest in Manik's discourse.

Manik saw the effect hitting the target. His eyes became widened. He continued, "Yes Sir, the Chairman of the Board of Control Mr. Wood Sahib".

-"What did he do?"

-"He had despatched his views on the education policy in 1854 to the then Governor General Lord Dalhousie, that is the Magna Carta of English Education in India."

-"Magna Carta? What is in that?"

-"That prescribes opening of Primary Vernacular Schools in villages, Anglo-Middle Schools and colleges in districts. In addition, that also prescribes the appointment of a Director of

Education in every province under whom will work the Department of Education."

-"Has any work been done in that direction?"

-"Surely, Lord Dalhousie himself worked on this in 1856."

-"Lord Dalhousie? You mean the Governor General?"

-"Yes."

-"And then?" All these sounded both strange and interesting to William Sahib. All these were new to him. He had started enjoying these talks. He had only enjoyed the trade and land so far. He liked also the war, which helped him amass wealth. He had enjoyed driving away Mr. Pierre and capturing his Bungalow. He had enjoyed grabbing all the land of Haji Hazrat Zafar Ali and driving him away. He had enjoyed making Raja Samman Singh a popper and securing all his land.

But he had never paid any attention to education. No one had told him about these. The British did so many great things for India just for education!

-"And then?" He remarked almost involuntarily.

-"Then", Manik found William Sahib getting interested and he was himself encouraged, "Mr. Charles Wood had told that in India universities like the University of London should also be opened."

-"These universities were not only opened but the British government also gave grants", added Mohan Mani.

-"Oh! They even gave grants", William Sahib looked at Mohan Mani in awe and with amazed looks. He was surprised because Mohan Mani is a soft-spoken and grave person. He speaks very little but whatever he speaks is always a truth and carries weight. He never speaks anything which is not the truth. It is he who introduced the Charkha (spinning wheel) in this village. It is he who organises and leads the Swadeshi movement. It is his command that all the labourers, farmers and other workers in the Estate and in the village obey without questioning. He is respected in the entire locality. He should never be antagonised. He asked, "What do you people want?"

-"We want an English medium school in this village", Mohan Mani said with great expectation. "That school will be called Williams English School".

-"What is this Williams?" was the question from William Sahib.

-"The school will be named after you. Your name will be etched in history forever. You will become famous and will be respected by all. People will talk about you always in future."

-"Daddy", Peterson interrupted, "The proposal is very good."

-"Is it really so?"

-"Yes."

-"What have I to do?" William Sahib was getting encouraged by his son's support.

William Sahib had so far known only "Taking". Take his land, take his house, take his life, take their wealth, take their labourers and the like. He knew how to take land. He knew how to take over the entire zamindari. But he never had any experience of "giving". That there is a different kind of pleasure and happiness in giving he had never experienced.

He now came to know about giving. It was a new kind of pleasure for him. He felt pleased with the happiness of Annie at the acceptance of her proposal. He was pleased with the way his son had supported him. He was pleased with the contented faces of the young leader Manik and the elderly leader Mohan Mani.

-"Actually" Manik had elaborated further, "There is some wasteland in the east of Haji Tola. On a two-acre plot of that land, a building with about ten rooms should be constructed. That's all. The school shall start functioning."

-"Shall start functioning?" William Sahib asked and said, "It would give me immense pleasure and more than that my daughter Annie would be pleased. She had been requesting us for so many months but we never paid any heed to her proposal, thinking it would be a waste of the effort. She actually enjoys doing such philanthropic acts. Her mother also enjoyed it. Do you know? Her mother came from the same Irish family from which came Dr. Grierson. I always praise the Irish blood. That's why I accept your proposal according to the wishes of my daughter."

William Sahib had turned his gaze towards his daughter and smiled.

That he smiled was a matter of great surprise. Surprise because no one had ever seen William Sahib smiling, neither his son and daughter nor any servants and other workers. He never expresses what he likes or dislikes. He does not speak. He is not used to expressing his views in any manner. Just keeps quiet.

Keeps quiet and works for his Estate, doggedly and single-mindedly. His mission – drive away Mr. Pierre, other mission – grab Haji Hazrat Zafar Ali's land and so on and so forth.

Now he saw the security of his Estate in the proposal for school. He gave his consent.

Tea was served once more after this. In between, Pincot had appeared there with Mary three times and gone.

Annie remained watching. Manik was not pleased with the undisciplined manner and unruliness of that man.

Annie had gone down to the gate to see Manik and Mohan Mani off. At the gate, Manik had asked, "Who is this person?"

-"Pincot."

-"What is he doing?"

-"He is a student."

-"But he is an unruly character." And both had crossed the gate.

*

Annie had reached the school gate by the time her chain of thought came to an end.

The gardener ran to the gate and saluted her.

There is a big lawn after the gate. The garden is set by the side of the lawn. The lawn is thick with grass. Then comes the school building - cement floor, brick wall and tin roof.

The classes were going on. Annie went to the office first. She sat on the chair, opened the drawer, pulled a piece of paper and began writing the leave application for the day.

The school caretaker Gopal stood by her side in attention.

Has the Headmaster arrived? Annie asked Gopal while folding the application up.

-"Yes Ma'am."

The Headmaster, Pandit Trilochan Jha Shastri, Kavyateerth, Ayurvedacharya, was earlier the Head Pandit of Purnia Zila School. He came back to the village after retirement. He was caught again for teaching.

He was lying on a cot on his *dalan*[5] that day. Two of his pupils were massaging his thighs and legs. He was busy enjoying tobacco snuff from a bottle.

Annie arrived just then with Manik and Mohan Mani.

-"Please come", he welcomed them and pointing to another cot nearby, asked them to sit there. He suddenly asked, "She is Annie, if I am not wrong."

-"Yes", Annie replied politely.

-"I have heard a lot about your philanthropic and social activities. Your love for education and social service is praiseworthy. I bless you heartily for your success and long life. I'm sorry, I don't have a chair to offer you."

-"Please do not worry Sir, I am used to sitting on the cot."

-"Another feather in your cap. You are really great."

---

[5] *Dalan:* An outhouse used by menfolk and guests in the villages, usually having a large courtyard, open veranda and a threshing yard, cattle shed etc.

-"Thanks a lot. It is all because of the blessings of elders like you and the love of villagers."

-"Is the school building ready?"

-"Yes, Sir. In fact, we have come to you to discuss something only about that."

-"Please order."

-"No order Sir, please cooperate, this is our earnest request."

-"My cooperation! You always have it. Just tell me what I need to do."

-"Kindly accept the position of Headmaster."

-"Now? Isn't it too late for me? I am retired."

-"No Sir, you have a long experience of Purnia Zila School. This is exactly what we need to start the school in a proper manner. We need a learned and experienced person like you."

-"But now ... in any case I shall consider myself fortunate to serve the society in any manner I can. You all are actually working for us only, this village, our society."

But that day Pandit Trilochan Jha Shastri was not spared. He had to accept the post of Headmaster of the new school. Old in knowledge, old in age.

The only weak point is that he cannot reach the school in time. Engaged in his daily chores of puja and all that. But otherwise he is an expert teacher, very strict and able administrator.

Annie looked at the wall clock. One O'clock. Tiffin time.

Gopal went to the veranda and rang the bell. Hardly fifteen to twenty students in all the classes put together. They came out of the classrooms and began playing on the lawn.

Many students do not join this school. The boys from Brahman Tola do not come, they attend the Tola Pathashala (local Sanskrit school), the boys from Rajput families do not come as they do not want to sit along with the boys of

Chamartoli and *Dusadhtoli*. Boys from *Chamartoli* and *Dusadhtoli* do not come as they don't need to study.

There is an overall aversion to this school. They teach English and everyone will become Christians like the British. They will lose their religion. Padri Sahib came; he divided the society and made a Christian Tola. Now William Sahib has opened this school to make more Christians.

There are so many different reasons for everyone, for guardians not to send their children to this new school. But the main reason is the fear of bodily contact with the untouchables and losing one's religion.

Headmaster Shastriji and Mohan Mani entered the staff room almost simultaneously. Even though Mohan Mani spent most of his time in other constructive social work like the Charkha and Swaraji Movement, he agreed to give some time to the school also as a purely voluntary work. He is also the secretary of the school. He said, "Annie, today you were to teach English. As you got delayed, I engaged the class in your place."

Annie replied, "Oh thank you so much. Suddenly I became busy with family affairs. I have brought the leave application for today."

-"What type of family affairs?" By that time Manik also entered the room. He asked, "Learnt that last night Pincot suddenly disappeared. Was it about that?"

-"You are right. We were busy searching for him but to no avail."

Annie realised the sarcasm in what Manik said. She smiled and added, "Wasn't it necessary? If suddenly one of your guests disappears without any information, will you not be worried?"

-"Surely", Manik was not to let it go, "And that too if the guest happens to be so special."

Manik's face, always dignified, had become a shade darker because of implicit sarcasm.

Mohan Mani said, "Whatever might be the reason, it is good that you are submitting a leave application. This will set a healthy trend. But at present the burning question before us is the future of the school."

-"And the future depends on how we attract more students", added Pandit Trilochan Jha Shastri, who was the only paid teacher among them, and he took out a little snuff from his pouch to stuff it into his nose.

Manik asked, "Panditji, how much has your own efforts succeeded?"

-"Not much, I went around the entire Tola. The people, particularly in my Tola, have some reservation."

-"What's that?" Mohan Mani asked.

-"First, having the children of the people, whom Mahatma Gandhi calls *Harijan*, sitting together with those of the upper castes in school will be tantamount to throwing the caste system away. So they are opposing it."

-"And the second?"

-"Teaching of English. People are afraid that teaching English will make their children Christians. They consider it a conspiracy in disguise of education. Once Padri Sahib made Christians and now William Sahib has jumped into that game."

-"But where is William Sahib in this?"

-"Why not? He gave the land, he gave money to construct the building. His daughter is a teacher ... what more does one need as proof?"

-"Do you also have doubts?"

-"Why should I have doubts?"

-"Then let us go and explain to them the real purpose."

-"That I am doing regularly. The day before yesterday I had been to the Pathashala. Some pupils along with the teacher Vyakaranacharya Dharmadhar Jha were sitting near the haystack. A few of the pupils were massaging his legs."

-"Why near the haystack?"

-"It seems you have not visited the Brahman Tola recently. A portion of the mud-built wall of the Pathashala fell down. A portion of the roof has also been damaged and has fallen down. The other roof is about to go down as well. There is another doubt among them."

-"What?"

-"Making children of all castes sit together, they think it is a conspiracy to remove their caste system and further by giving English education and making people Christians, take away the religion also. In addition, the teachers are afraid of losing their jobs."

-"Why the fear of losing jobs?"

-"There are only two teachers in the Pathashala. They are being paid Five rupees per month as salary. If the students leave, they are afraid the Board will stop paying their salary."

-"Should we give them some assurance?" Manik asked.

-"Sure", Annie replied, "They can come to our school and continue teaching Sanskrit there. Only a few periods we shall engage for English language, mathematics, history and geography etc.

-"I have explained this many times. But ..."

-"We should go and explain to the guardians also". Mohan Mani said. Everyone thought for a while. In the meantime, the bell rang.

Annie returned to the Bungalow much before sunset. Before entering the gate she looked at the Kothi Bazaar.

The Bazaar was full of people. Different voices from so many people created noise of a peculiar kind. Sale and purchase were in full swing. People thronged the shops.

But, the office of Manager Mr. Sanyal was closed. The rooms of Badri Gumasta and Giridhari Das were also closed. Annie was puzzled.

Soon as she entered the gate, she found the answer. Peterson was holding his court on the lawn.

It is known that the court is held here on the lawn, a little towards the left, where there is an elevated platform.

Earlier William Sahib used to sit on this very platform. On one side would be sitting on chairs the Manager and the Assistant Manager. On the other side on a carpet would be sitting the clerk Badri Gumasta and the accountant Giridhari Das with his bag. Standing behind would be the retinue of lower-rung servants, peons, orderlies, watchmen, caretakers, cart drivers and the like. The petitioner farmer tenants would be standing below the platform in front of them.

On the right side, there were several five-foot tall poles erected for special purposes.

Rouge tenants would be tied to one of these poles and would be whipped. They would be whipped till they bled and then chilli powder would be sprayed over the wounds. Other tenants, the onlookers, would watch it terrified. Sometimes when William Sahib would become very angry, he himself would take the whip.

William Sahib has now grown old. These are stories of yesteryears. Stories of the time when William Sahib was a young man and Annie was a small child.

Annie was a child, and so many things she does not recall.

But the handless Ramy Jamadar remembers every detail of those days. He also remembers the struggles of William Sahib in his early days. The incidence of Mr. Pierre quitting the village leaving the Bungalow behind, taking possession of land belonging to Haji Hazrat Zafar Ali, annexing the zamindaris, the incidences connected with the festivals, strong administration and above all those of William Sahib getting angry and then beating people. During those days ten poles had been erected, side by side. Up to ten rogue tenants could be punished simultaneously, the punishment depending on the nature of the crime.

He recalls an incident when William Sahib had got so angry that he had tied five tenants to the poles at the same time and the sepoys began beating each one of them. Even the poles had become blood red. The offenders would be crying in pain, but the sepoys would throw more salt and chilli powder on their wounds. Their family members would watch in stunned silence in grief. No one dared speak. Protesting meant more beating.

Ramy Jamadar vividly recalls all such incidents. He tells these stories to Annie once in a while....

While crossing the lawn Annie noticed that Peterson was sitting on a chair on the platform. Beside him also were sitting the Manager Mr. Sanyal, the Assistant Manager Mr. Singh and Badri Gumasta. The accountant Giridhari Das was sitting with his books open. Other minions were standing behind.

But no tenant was tied to a pole today. The farmer tenants were sitting on the ground in front. The court was in session.

Further on she found that the party was in full swing in the main drawing room. Kebabs and other savouries were served on plates on the table, as were the drinks srrved in the glasses on the table. The New Year picnic party was in full swing with the cook Rahman, butler Hamid and bearer Dinu at service.

-"Hello Annie, where had you been?", Tony addressed her.

-"To the School."

-"Oh school, college, India, Indian culture, I am bored with hearing these things for so long here."

-"I am sorry that you are offended", Annie smiled.

-"Yes. We all are offended. Look, neither Peterson nor you have been here. What are the guests to do without a host?"

-"Sorry... very sorry."

-"It's a matter of great concern to us. By opening a school here you have become so busy as if you were opening Oxford

University. You are spoiling yourself among the black rustic natives."

-"Why?", Annie sat down, "Aren't they human beings?"

-"Of course not, they are animals. You are running after animals here and spoiling yourself."

-"It seems you have forgotten to distinguish between humans and animals under the influence of alcohol."

-"Not me, Annie, you have forgotten the difference between humans and animals. Just because someone has hands and feet does not make him a human being. If that were so, even Chimpanzees and Gorillas would qualify to be humans."

-"Note down Tony that the day these Chimpanzees and Gorillas will get hands and feet, that day you will not be sitting and drinking as comfortably." Annie had become a bit angry.

-"Then?"

-"Then, you will have to return to that land from where you came here. All these merry-making will come to an end. You may not get time even to pack your belongings or meet your friends."

-"Thanks. But mark my words that the British, that great British will not have to see that day,. .. at least till the descendants of some Mir Zafars, some Raja Manik Chand and some Ray Durlabh stay alive in this country."

-"This means you have forgotten 1857 and have forgotten the bitter experiences of Havelock, Campbell and Nicholson."

-"They did have some bad experiences but you are also probably forgetting that those were momentary and after that, the way Indians had been beaten and their movements crushed. You also forget what General Dyer did in Lahore in 1919."

-"Pity, the incident which brought shame to England should become a topic of pride for you."

-"Why should it be a matter of shame?"

-"The barbaric mass killing of innocents brought a permanent scar on the British race and British society. It will remain etched in history as the most shameful acts which history will never forgive."

-"Listen Annie", Pit, nephew of the Collector of Bhagalpur, remarked after keeping his glass on the table with a thud, "You are unnecessarily becoming emotional. This is not a question of emotion but of history. Such incidents are very insignificant, negligible for the race which creates history."

-"What do you mean?" Annie retorted.

-"The meaning is evident. The great English race is creating a new era in history in this miserable and filthy India. The English are bringing Indians out of the darkness onto the pedestal of light. They are converting them from uncivilised to civilised, from conservative to progressive. They are giving Indians the eyes of education. They are teaching them the essence of science. They are bringing here the prosperity with industrial revolution. They are transforming the society from an indisciplined one to a disciplined one with strict administration."

-"Absolutely." It was Tony again responding. "The Indians should always be grateful to the English. Macaulay gave them education, Stephenson gave them rail transportation, Warren Hastings brought order to a completely disoriented society and Lord Cornwallis gave them administration. Everything was given by the English. What did India have?"

-"It's difficult to talk with you people." Annie got irritated. "There is a difference between scholarly discussion and forced argumentation. But remember: When your entire Europe was in the ice age, India had already entered the metal age. During the period when Europeans were still fighting as barbaric, India had a developed civilization. England will have to learn Humaneness and Decency from Indians. The popular uprising called democracy which happened in England in 1688 had its roots in

India millennia ago. And the so-called modern Industrial developments you people boast of, thank India again that it took place in England."

-"Right, you have become a blind Orientalist." Pit added.

-"One should have", Annie replied, cutting short Pit in the middle, "the humility and discretion to accept Truth as Truth. Imagine, if the English had not plundered India fraudulently, had the Industrial Revolution taken place so rapidly in England? Had the pace of the Industrial Revolution not been rapid, would your society have become prosperous? Had the progress of scientific developments been the same? Would they have been able to establish such a huge empire? ... It is England which should be grateful to India."

-"You are wonderful, Annie."

-"Annie is not wonderful", Jennie, daughter of the Collector of Purnia, who had been listening silently so far, finally blurted out, "Wonderful are you people that for so long all of you have been fighting with a single woman and that too without any reason. You all have spoiled a happy evening. Go ahead with your drinks. Annie, I guess you have a special programme this evening."

And taking Annie's hands Jennie came out of the main drawing room.

While walking away from the drawing room Jennie said, "Annie, sometimes you get excited unnecessarily."

-"Why don't they talk meaningful things?"

-"They are not capable of doing so."

-"Thanks."

Annie entered her wing. Roopy had been waiting.

-"Roopy, get some tea quickly and ask for the palanquin."

-"What for?" Jennie asked.

-"For you."

-"For me?"

-"Yes, you had told me that you would accompany me to the Guruji's house."

-"I am eager."

-"But you must pay him your respect properly, in the traditional Indian style". She looked at Jennie.

-"What does that mean?"

-"That means leaning and touching his feet."

-"Agreed."

-"Do not talk of any drinks there."

-"Surely I shall not do anything like that. It's only for that I touched no liquor at all since this afternoon."

-"Also, you will not smoke."

-"Agreed, but can't I smoke while coming out?"

-"No."

-"Any other condition?"

-"Be dignified."

-"Shall try. First, let me have a look at your Guruji."

Jennie smiled. Annie shook her chin and looking at the sweater lying on the bed, went to her room inside.

Jennie began looking at the sweater by turning it over from side to side. It was a pullover, of fine knitting. She had seen Annie knitting this with great care and concentration. She had thought it was meant for Pincot, but when he had left, she asked Annie about it.

-"It was not for Pincot."

-"Then for Peterson?"

-"No."

-"Then for whom? Which Englishman is so lucky?"

-"No Englishman at all."

-"Then is it for an Indian? Who is that fortunate man?"

-"I have knitted it for Manik." Annie had given an elaborate introduction of Manik to Jennie after that.

Elaboration was also made by Roopy, for the palanquin. In recent days Annie had stopped using the palanquin. She used to take the *sampani* cart. No one else likes *sampani* cart. Neither William Sahib nor Peterson.

Peterson prefers horses. He usually rides horses. If not, then a palanquin. He has a separate palanquin.

William Sahib also likes palanquin, especially now after he has grown old. He also used to ride horses earlier. He used to ride to various parts of his Estate; while going to ... farming camps, to oversee indigo cultivation, while going to take tenants to task and the like. But now he uses only the palanquin. His and Peterson's palanquins are always kept clean, shining and ready.

But Annie's palanquin is not in a serviceable condition as it is not used frequently. When Roopy requisitioned the palanquin, the servants got into action. Roopy asked Dinu to get it ready. Dinu has always liked Annie sitting inside the palanquin. He imagines her as a newly married bride going to her husband's house. While getting into the palanquin, Annie looks like a bride. Oh, when will she get married? She is already so old. Why doesn't she get married? Had she got married, by now she would have given birth to at least a couple of children. Dinu thinks traditionally.

It is sad that married for such a long time he does not have a child himself. He tried many tricks, from local herbal remedies to the treatment by sorcerers and Pandits. But to no avail. He is an unhappy man.

But he becomes happy while watching Annie enter a palanquin. She has not used the palanquin for long. He does not know if it is at all dusted and clean. If it is not clean he will see to it the bearers get punished. He will get back the land they have. It's only then that they will realise their mistakes. They have been enjoying a free food and no work. They just lie down and while away their time. They forget their main duty is to keep the palanquin always ready for use.

Dinu's requisition set into motion a chain reaction among various levels of servants down to the palanquin bearers. But by that time Annie had changed her mind. She will take the *sampani* cart. Dinu ran again.

Roopy brought tea in the meantime. Annie came out.

-"Annie, the pullover has come out excellent. Will you carry it now?" Jennie asked while Roopy served her tea.

-"Whatever your wish."

-"How does it matter? If I say do not take it, will you agree?"

-"Yes, I shall not take it then."

-"Why should I commit such an atrocious act?"

-"It's no atrocity", Annie smiled.

-"Very much. A lot of sweet memories of Manik are knitted into this sweater. Why should I interfere with your happiness? On the contrary, I have another proposal."

-"What?"

-"That I should not accompany you; you go alone so that you can give it to him in private."

-"You please take this idea out of your head that there is anything very private between the two of us. Our relationship is based on public good. Nothing personal there. And don't think that this gift means any personal feelings. You will see it for yourself. .. Are you ready? ...But what's this?" Annie was taken aback a bit.

-"What?" Jennie looked at her with a question mark.

-"You are in a blouse and skirt."

-"Can't I go there in this dress?"

-"Of course ... you can." Annie thought for a moment and then added, "Let us go. Panditji is a great soul; he is not a narrow-minded and conservative one. He doesn't care for all these things."

-"I got it."

-"What?"

-"The question of contrast. But that will benefit you."

-"How?"

-"See, first you objected to my wearing a blouse and a skirt. Your natural choice was that I should also wear the Indian dress, a sari, like you. But suddenly a prodigious thought came to you that it would make better sense to have a contrast. That will elevate you to an extraordinary level in the eyes of Panditji while I shall remain ordinary. Is this not a benefit for you?"

Annie looked sharply at Jennie. There was no malice on Jennie's face. She pulled Jennie's face and embracing her, kissed her. She kept sucking her lips for a few moments before releasing. Showing her appreciation, she said, "Jennie, your thought process has been so natural. Marvellous. You are not like Mary, so there is no malice or contempt on your face. You had yourself expressed the desire to meet Panditji. I had only given a hint. This hint I have given to so many people so many times. But no one agreed to go there in a purely non-vegetarian environment leaving the food and drinks here. You agreed and that's the first step of gaining knowledge. This is also an unnatural state which Panditji likes. So far as the advantage is concerned, it's yours." Annie continued smiling.

-"My advantage? How?"

-"Not one but two. The second is such that you will certainly be startled once you hear that."

-"Then please tell that quickly."

-"First, that you don't have to wear a sari. If at all you wore one, you would have to borrow from me, but that's against your principles. Second, you didn't need to change. That saved time. Also, wearing a sari is tricky and needs practice. If one is not sufficiently experienced, here is a chance it may slip away anywhere anytime. And God forbid if that happened in front of Panditji...."

-"Stop it!...." Jennie began laughing loudly and she embraced Annie tightly. She also kissed her.

*

Annie and Jennie arrived at the *dalan* of Pandit Motinath Jha in Brahman Tola well before it was dark in the evening. Annie knew the house and the locality well. She found Panditji sitting alone on his cot and understood that soon before it would be dark, several important people would begin arriving there for their evening gossip. In between there might be some family disputes to be settled of the villagers who approached them.

Panditji was known for settling disputes in the entire village. Usually, both parties would agree to whatever judgement would be pronounced. Pandit Motinath Jha is respected as the most learned and revered person for his unbiased and impartial views not only in the village of Dharampur but also around the locality.

He had been an accomplished scholar even in Kashi where he had his education and then spent his youth teaching in the famous Queen's College. He came back to Dharampur after retirement. Even though he had degrees only in Literature, Grammar and Ayurveda, he had equal command over Nyay (syllogism), Religious Literature and Vedic practices. During his days at the Queen's College, he was the only teacher who could engage the classes for almost all the disciplines apart from his own specializations. He always satisfied the students' curiosity. He was also qualified in Astrology.

Annie had explained everything about Panditji to Jennie while on their way. However, when they arrived, Jennie was more surprised. Surprised at the huge compound - the *dalan* with the adjoining threshing yard, the very wide veranda, the house constructed with thick wooden beams and rafts, the heaps of harvested paddy lying around, thrashed paddy heaps, the huge stack of hay kept like a mountain in another corner and the large number of farming accessories lying nearby.

Annie and Jennie climbed the three steps of bricks and mud, and reached the veranda. They stopped near the chairs kept there. Panditji was engrossed in some book. Finally, he looked around, and finding the two English ladies, pointed to the chairs for them to sit down. Jennie, following Annie, touched Panditji's feet and sat down on a chair. Annie, however, was surprised at the chairs. She had not seen chairs here earlier. She recalled her first visit to this place when the hosts had been embarrassed at her inability to sit on a cot, and had provided for her a make-shift seat of an inverted wooden *okhal*[6] with a cushion of a folded blanket over it. During several of her subsequent visits, this remained the practice. Although she eventually got used to sitting on a cot, being the lone female visitor, she could not occupy an entire cot and sharing it with other males was considered uncivilised. She asked Panditji, "It seems these chairs have been brought recently".

-"Yes, considering the inconveniences faced by you people, I got a carpenter from Purnia to make five chairs here. It has been quite some time since you visited us. I hope you are healthy and happy."

-"Yes, with your blessings and with God's grace, I am healthy but not very happy." Said Annie with a smile.

She had started speaking Hindi reasonably well, although not fluently. She needed a lot of practise. She has learnt the most in the school here, from both the pupils and the teachers. Sometimes she can also act as a bilingual interpreter.

---

[6] *Okhal :* the wooden mortar, typically the height of a stool, which is used in the household for milling paddy to get rice, pounding paddy to obtain Chiura, grinding spices etc.

Jennie was unable to understand a good part of the conversation between Panditji and Annie because of the language barrier. She had begun looking at the walls and the ceiling with exquisite beams and rafts.

Only two sides of the veranda had brick walls with a number of shelves recessed into them. The other two sides were wide open. On one side of a cot, there was a blanket spread and a bolster pillow kept, against which Panditji was leaning. On the other side, there were three cots in a row, all having blankets spread over them, behind the chairs also there was another cot with a blanket spread. At present all the cots were empty. There was enough gap between the cots for people to move around. Each cot near it had a *Lota* (metal water pot) on the floor. The ground on the entire veranda was clean, having been swept and mopped with a mixture of mud and cow dung. An air of serenity and peace prevailed all around.

Decency is a great virtue for Panditji himself - sixty-five to seventy years of age, very fair complexion, handsome and attractive. Carefully applied three parallel-lines of sandalwood paste, running from left to right, with a large circular dot of vermillion below it in the centre above the nose decorated his wide forehead. He is wearing a *Mirjai* on the body, has a string of *Rudraksha* around his neck and a shawl on his shoulders. His dress makes him look elegant, grave and elite. A book with a peacock feather as a bookmark is kept by the side of the bolster.

Jennie was impressed by the surrounding and the set-up there. The most significant was the air of purity and a serenity prevailing around.

When Jennie looked around, she found a labourer had come and stood near Panditji. Panditji gestured to him and he left. Annie recognized the person, he was the personal servant of Panditji.

-"Not very happy?" Panditji turned towards Annie. He shifted his position, sat upright and looked at her.

The darkness of early evening had begun to spread around slowly. It was getting cold as well.

-"You know Sir, I had to struggle hard with my family for opening an English medium school, apart from the existing Pathashala and the Madarsa. Now that we have the building and some teachers also, the number of students is not satisfactory."

-"I am well aware. I come to know of these problems through Manik and Pandit Trilochan Jha Shastri. But that we shall talk later. First, you introduce your friend."

Pandit Motinath Jha looked at Jennie. Jennie became conscious and pulled her skirt over her knees as far down as it allowed. She could somehow follow what Annie spoke but had difficulty comprehending the words spoken by Panditji. Just now when Panditji talked about her, she understood what it meant. That's why she was alert now.

Annie introduced Jennie using some more English words for her friend's convenience. She emphasized that her friend also had a liking for Indian culture and traditions. That was the reason she wanted to visit him.

Jennie looked at the contended face of Panditji and she again saluted him in the manner taught by Annie. She then asked Panditji about the ancient Indian culture and traditions. Annie explained her questions.

Panditji was very happy with her curiosity and the questions put forth. He replied, "See, your question is very important and the answer is also quite long. But I shall try to summarize it in brief as the evening is getting cold."

-"You needn't worry Sir. We have blankets with the orderly in the *sampani* cart." Annie explained.

-"Blankets can be provided here also." Saying this Panditji's son Manik and his friend Mohan Mani joined and occupied the remaining two chairs there.

-"Thanks a lot. Actually cold is not a problem, the problem is the time and the topic of discussion."

-"Sorry, we interrupted. Please excuse us and continue the discussion."

Saying this Manik smiled. Others also smiled but Panditji became grave. He became grave at the manner Annie and his son Manik exchanged glances. But there was another interruption.

A servant brought a small bathing table and kept it between Panditji's cot and the row of chairs. Another person brought a waterpot with water and two glasses and a third person brought two plates with some biscuits in them and two glasses having hot tea.

Manik hinted to one of the servants and quickly a couple of glasses of tea were brought. Manik himself and Mohan Mani each took tea of those two glasses.

Annie took the water pot, went to the edge of the veranda close to the eaves and washed her hands there. Jennie followed her and did exactly what Annie had done. They returned to their seats and began to eat the biscuits and take tea.

In the meantime some five to seven villagers came and took their seats on the cots kept around. Some more villagers including Pandit Trilochan Jha Shastri, the Headmaster of the English School, also came and took their seats.

Soon a lantern was hung in the eaves. In addition, three four-headed earthen lamps filled with castor oil were also brought and kept on their stands at suitable places on the veranda for light. One of these lamps was kept between the chairs of Annie and Jennie and Panditji's cot. There was now sufficient light around to beat the darkness. The atmosphere was, however, quiet and heavy in spite of so many people present there.

Jennie reminded Panditji, "My question, Sir."

-"Your curiosity is praiseworthy." Panditji remarked with satisfaction, "See, according to the archaeologists the Indian civilization is some ten thousand years old, since the time they began finding burnt and rotten grains and other artefacts. But obviously, a civilization was born the day when people left hunting-gathering and began animal husbandry leaving their cave-dwelling and began constructing clusters of settlements. Agriculture enters at a later stage in such a society at a slow pace. That stage would have commenced approximately five thousand years before that ten-thousand-year period which archaeologists determine. In this way, we find that the Indian civilization is some fifteen thousand years old. It's a different matter that there is no archaeological evidence for the previous five thousand years as yet. Still, the ten-thousand-year-old Indian civilization is considered the oldest civilization in the world." Panditji narrated it all in one breath and looked at the faces of Annie and Jennie and also at others sitting there.

Realizing that Jennie had difficulty comprehending the entire conversation due to language problems, Annie explained to her in plain English what Panditji told.

The assemblage at the veranda found the English translation incomprehensible and boring after listening to the profound discourse of Panditji. However, Manik and Mohan Mani, being versed in English, had no such issues.

Jennie's eyes brightened after listening to Annie's translation. She asked the next question, "And what about the other civilizations, in particular our European one?"

-"Europe's civilization may be considered some five thousand years old, China's some seven thousand years old, Egypt about eight thousand years old, and rest of Asia around ten thousand years old."

Jennie felt a bit of an inferiority complex while others sitting around felt proud. Annie knew all this, so she too felt proud.

-"And what is the history of culture?" Jennie put her next question.

-"Asia is quite developed in this area also. Indian Dravidian culture is almost contemporary with   Mesopotamian and

Babylonian civilizations. These cultures had travel and trade relations also, for which evidence has emerged. Later we encounter the Greek, Chinese and finally the Roman civilizations. The ages for Egyptian and Asian civilizations happen to be around six thousand years before Christ and all others are the later evolutions."

Panditji took a moment's break and looked at Annie and Jennie. Jennie was awestruck. Her respect for Panditji was growing by the minute which Panditji also felt. Everyone present there including Annie was listening to the speech in rapt attention.

Panditji was encouraged by the attention of the audience and further said, "Let me give you an example. Jesus Christ, whom you worship, and the religion of Christianity were born in Asia, do you agree? You also know that the so-called Christian era started from the day of the assumed birth of Christ."

-"Yes", Jennie responded.

-"Even in Rome, Christianity spread only four hundred years later. It was first adopted by the people of Constantinople in the Turkish part of the Eastern Roman Empire. Earlier, whoever adopted Christianity in the Western Roman Empire was persecuted in multiple ways. The religion spread to other parts of Europe only after its foothold was established in the Western Roman Empire regions."

-"And what is the status of literature?" Jennie was impressed by the depth of Panditji's knowledge.

-"In the realm of literature, India has been at the forefront not only in Asia but in the entire world. The world's first literature, the Rigveda, was composed in India. This is actually the first conscious human's song. This is acknowledged by all the Indologists, Orientalists and historians alike." Said Panditji and began wiping his spectacles.

-"Good that the subject is under discussion today." Annie joined the discourse animatedly, "Last time there was an interruption and my questions had remained unanswered."

-"Which question?" Panditji looked smilingly at Annie.

-"Sir, you may not remember. My question was regarding the ancient Indian literature."

-"Oh yes, I recall now." Panditji became grave and thought for a minute. He told something to Manik in Maithili which the two English ladies did not understand. Manik got up and left.

Quickly a servant brought two blankets and handed them over to the English guests. He returned back to sit near the bonfire. Manik came back and took his original seat. Another servant came and adjusted the wicks of the lamps.

-"I recall your question now", Panditji began after some thought, "Although the answer is rather long, I shall try to give a brief account, if you have time."

-"Yes Sir, there is plenty of time." Annie replied.

-"In the year 1651 two important events happened", Panditji said with all seriousness, "One in England and another here in India. In England, the language of the parliament and the judiciary, which was French till 1650, became English for the first time in 1651. In the same year in India, the foundation for research in ancient Indian culture and literature was laid down by a Dutch priest named Abraham Roger. He was the first to make a list of Indian Brahman treatises and translate some of the couplets on policy matters written by Bhartrihari. Some fifty years later another Jesuit priest worked on the Sanskrit Grammar which was published by an Austrian priest. Actually only after the works of these priests came to light within Europe that Warren Hastings and Sir William Jones undertook many monumental works which led to increased interest among Europeans about the ancient Indian literature. Sir William Jones established the Asiatic Society to work on the Oriental literature and Lord Hastings employed several scholars of Sanskrit to work as juries in court proceedings using their knowledge of the *Smriti* treatises of legal subjects. He also directed several English scholars towards Sanskrit and sent some of them to Kashi to learn the language there, prominent among them being Charles Wilkins. Charles Wilkins translated a number of Sanskrit texts into English and published them. He also devised the typeset for the Devnagri script (the script used in Sanskrit writing) which is an important event in history. Later in this series, H.T. Colebrook produced original works, in addition to the translation, publication and compilation of a large repertoire of available texts comprising subjects like Nyay (syllogism), Religion, Philosophy, Literature, Grammar, Astrology and Mathematics. All these culminated in the heightened interest among scholars in Europe, especially among the French, German and even English scholars and specialists in Oriental studies. These scholars began searching for experts for Sanskrit within their fields to teach them Sanskrit and some even made plans to visit India. Charles Wilkins and Alexander Hamilton, the learned Sanskrit scholars had returned to England. While Wilkins stayed in England, Hamilton went to live in France where he was briefly interned. The demand for Sanskrit learning was such that German poet Karl Schlegel went to meet Alexander Hamilton in the French jail to learn Sanskrit from him. This led to greater interest among German scholars in Indian literature and the Germans made important contributions to Oriental studies. As the translations by German and French scholars gained pace, the Europeans in general became curious about Indian literature."

Panditji paused briefly and looked around, in particular towards the two English ladies. Everyone was listening in rapt attention and looking at the speaker with awe and reverence.

Satisfied with the effect of his discourse on the audience, he continued, "But the Europeans really were shaken out of slumber with the publication of the translation of *Upanishads* by the French scholar Abraham Anquetil-Duperron. European scholars had not encountered any work having such deep thought, detailed logical reasoning and sublime contemplation before this. After that during the entire Nineteenth century, Europe saw a flood of translation and publication of Indian literature and philosophical treatises. A number of important writings, compilations, editing and publications followed. A number of famous European universities began courses in Sanskrit studies. Noted European scholars contributed immensely to understanding the Vedic literature and Indian philosophy, a trend which continues till today. Several Indian scholars also made significant contributions, important among them being Raja Ram Mohan Roy and later Pandit Bal Gangadhar Tilak."

While Panditji was still speaking, a servant brought two plates of lightly fried *Chiura* and deep-fried *Tilkora*[7] leaves. Another servant brought two glasses of water and one full water pot and kept them on the small table kept there.

Annie was familiar with the eatables. But Jennie being unfamiliar asked Annie about the items served. Annie explained it to her and asked her to follow her.

Jennie went and washed her hands as Annie did, wiped her hands with a handkerchief and took the plate. She had been trying to understand the discourse, asking questions wherever necessary and the more she grasped the subject, the greater became her happiness and her admiration for the scholarship of Panditji.

Everyone present at the veranda was looking with curiosity at Annie and Jennie trying to eat the stuff from the plate. While Annie could easily manage eating *Chiura* with her hand, Jennie was struggling. She just could not take enough in her hand and put it into her mouth, her hand would go astray while trying. This made a hilarious sight for the onlookers who were laughing.

---

[7] *Tilkora :* Mithila's very own speciality, leaves of a special creeper grown there, these are deep fried after mixing with a paste of rice or sometimes also gram powder.

Jennie felt ashamed and blushed at her failure. But Annie was trying her best to teach her the proper way.

In between something unexpected happened. Suddenly twenty-odd people, old and young, arrived there from Jolaha (weavers) Tola. They stood near the edge of the veranda. Most of them kept their hands folded as if pleading. Panditji was a bit taken aback, some felt alarmed.

But Mohan Mani and Manik immediately knew why they came. They knew the problems faced by Jolahas in that village. Manik gestured for them to sit on the carpet spread on the veranda. Most of the people sat on the carpet but some old fellows did not sit. They remained standing with hands folded, expressing their grief.

Mohan Mani and Manik shifted their chairs to get a view of the newcomers and listen to what they had to say. Annie and Jennie also shifted their chairs.

Panditji asked them about their general well-being and the purpose of coming there so late in the evening.

One of the old men standing there began narrating the problems faced by their clan. He was speaking in Maithili and in between trying to wipe his eyes as well.

Everyone present there was listening to the tale of their suffering and feeling sad. Annie and Jennie were also listening but could not understand anything at all. The only words Annie could fathom were William Kutta (her father's slightly distorted name) and that of her brother Peterson. She understood that whatever was being said related to her family but more than that she could not make out.

The old man remained standing even after he had finished. The audience in silence felt pity. Panditji gestured for him to sit down and he obeyed.

Panditji looked at Mohan Mani and guessing what Panditji wanted, Mohan Mani in turn looked at Manik. Annie was also looking at Manik expectantly.

Manik began translating in English what the old man had narrated about their ordeal. The sum and substance was that during the early days of the expansion of his Estate, William Kutt had given these Jolahas homestead land for settlement and also cultivable land on rent for farming. He also encouraged them in various ways to retain their family traditions of weaving. Although William Kutta was known to be very cruel, his methods of punishment, even though one of the severest, were much milder in comparison to those employed by the previous Muslim Landlord whose land finally Kutta had managed to annex. He showed some sympathy towards these weavers so that some three-four families even embraced Christianity. Whatever the past, more recently there have been two incidents which have driven these people to almost destitution and if the situation does not improve, it may ultimately lead to their extinction.

The first is the onslaught of imported clothes. Since the days when markets in Purnia and Bhagalpur began stocking and selling imported English clothes, these weavers had lost almost all business. The clothes from England were soft and also more colourful which attracted customers. These clothes are so attractive that no one buys the coarse grey clothes woven locally by the weavers. Thus they lost all business.

The second, and much more grave, is the order of the new Master, Peterson, regarding their land. He has asked them to stop weaving and concentrate on indigo farming on whatever land they had. If they did not, their homestead land given by the Senior Kutt will be taken back. This has completely unsettled the Jolahas and they were on the verge of not only losing their trade but also their homestead. Both food and shelter gone, they would be forced to migrate to God knows where.

Forced into such a pitiable situation they had come to seek Annie Ma'am's intervention, knowing her kindness and love towards the natives. Only she can protect them. When they learnt that she had come here, they decided to meet her here, in the presence of others who might help them convey their tragic situation. They cannot even dream of going to Peterson Sahib's court seeking mercy.

After this translation, Manik looked around, giving a sharp glance at Annie, and sat down. Everyone sitting there became quiet and were filled with pity at the Jolahas' plight.

Annie thought for a brief while. Then she looked at Panditji and pointing towards the gathered Jolahas, she began in Hindi, "Everyone knows Peterson's obstinacy. My suggestion is to find a middle ground. I advise these people to agree to Indigo farming on part of the land and traditional agriculture on the rest. I shall try to convince my brother. But I can assure them right away that their homestead land will not be taken back. They can continue living in this village. As regards weaving, they can certainly continue with the trade but they will have to find a market for their clothes. No one can help them in this matter."

By and large everyone, including the Jolahas, was happy with this advice. Mohan Mani got up and thanking Annie, said, "We all know that imported mill clothes have been consigned to flame in mass uprising here. But without taking recourse to such an extreme step, I advise people to follow Gandhiji's principle of wearing homespun clothes, which now goes by its popular name Khadi. If everyone decides to wear Khadi, the problem of finding a market for weavers will be automatically solved."

This gave many sitting there a chance to consider wearing Khadi. They decided then and there that henceforth they would wear Khadi only. They would also try to convince many more to do so.

The atmosphere had by now turned from one of gloom to that of happiness. The Jolaha community paid Panditji their respects and thanking Annie profusely in their own characteristic way, departed from there.

A servant came and served fresh water and filled the pots. He then adjusted the wicks in the lamps. It was getting colder slowly as the night descended.

Panditji adjusted his blanket and said, "Annie, we are all grateful to you. I thank you and bless you as well. Today you showed your magnanimity and helped the Jolahas stay in the village. In fact, they got another life."

Annie was about to say something but Mohan Mani came forward and began, "Annie certainly deserves thanks from all of us. But in order to protect the Jolaha community, we need to propagate the word that more and more people should wear Khadi. This is a collective responsibility, not the work of an individual. We must do it together."

Those sitting there repeated their determination again to wear Khadi and also go around house to house in the village to propagate the word.

Mohan Mani added, "It is also necessary we all should take up spinning on Charkha as Gandhiji has pleaded. It is our duty to publicize this in every household and among all the women. In the near future, I plan to go to Bhagalpur District Office and bring some Charkha from there."

-"Why only among the women?" Pandit Trilochan Jha Shastri asked, "We all can spin thread using Charkha. We also should do our bit."

There were many voices from the crowd, "Yes, we can do, we shall do."

-"Most welcome, Mohan Mani added, "If we all decide to spin and wear Khadi, certainly the use of imported cloths will substantially come down and our weavers will get the desired market. When that happens, then only the dream of Pandit Jawahar Lal Nehru about total freedom, which he announced in the Lahore Congress last year, will come to fruition."

Everyone was excited. Annie stood from her seat and announced, "Only today did I realize the full potential of the

Charkha and Khadi movement initiated by Mahatma Gandhi. My wholehearted support for that. I appeal to Mohan Mani and Manik Jha that they should bring one Charkha for me also. I shall also learn spinning and I also decide to use only Khadi cotton henceforth like any Indian woman."

Seeing Mohan Mani and Manik begin clapping, everyone followed in a loud applause on the veranda. Everyone praised the dedication of Annie towards education, the village, and the Indian culture and tradition.

-"But for that, Annie will have to go to an Indian household and learn Charkha", Mohan Mani said smilingly.

-"No problem, I will. I am quite familiar with an Indian household in this village. The only problem may be of the language. I request Manikji to help me with that", Annie replied again with a smile.

-"I shall be very happy to do that", Manik quickly added.

Suddenly something happened. As it was getting late and growing cold, two orderlies arrived from the Kothi. Annie asked them to sit around the bonfire for some time and began to discuss the issues faced by her school with Panditji. The main concern was the highly inadequate number of children.

-"The number may further dwindle", Pandit Trilochan Jha Shastri declared.

-"Why?" A number of people joined to ask.

Everyone looked at him.

It is Shastriji's habit to arouse excitement among the listeners before he clarifies his point. He became grave and then continued, "Haji Sahib of Muslim Tola was telling him that he wants to start a Madarsa where the children of the eastern Muslim Tola will also come and get education. He has already got an assurance from Mr. William Kutt for assistance. But there is one problem he faces…"

He paused and looked around without completing his sentence.

-"What problem?" Mohan Mani asked in expectation.

-"The Muslim guardians do not agree."

Shastriji finished in a hurry as it was getting late. He opened his snuff box. Several comments came from different quarters on this issue. In the end, Manik began summarizing the event, "We too face somewhat similar problem. We have to go around each household and convince the guardians. We shall do that.... See Annieji, we three have discussed these issues many times among us. Each section of society has its own traditional educational system. That has to be allowed to continue at least for some time. And when people begin to realize the benefits of job-oriented education, like it has happened in Bombay (now called Mumbai), Madras, and Calcutta which led to the growth of students in English schools, the students would begin to join our school also. This will automatically reduce the importance of Tola Pathashala and Madarsa. We should not be disappointed. On the contrary, we should keep doing our hard work and try to convince the guardians. The future is ours." Manik got up and added further, "Even though it is against the culture of Mithila to bring a meeting to an end and ask the guests to go home, I am compelled to do so as it is now quite late. It is time for Mohan Mani to take milk and the orderlies are waiting here for our English guests."

-"Thank you", Annie said with great satisfaction, "I am really happy that the evening was quite fruitful in many respects, in particular concerning the exposition of ancient Oriental knowledge and literature. I must thank the host for the very special snacks we had. This is enough to bring us back here again and again and in that process, I shall also learn spinning. Thank you all again."Annie and Jennie got up and departed.

Everyone followed. The orderlies ran to follow the ladies.

Mohan Mani and Manik went to see the ladies off to some distance. Jennie had climbed the *sampani* cart but Annie kept walking. While Mohan Mani returned after going some distance, Manik continued to walk along with Annie following the cart.

Suddenly Annie stopped.

The orderlies were at some distance ahead. She whispered, "Oh, I had completely forgotten about the sweater. This is for you". And she gave the sweater to Manik.

In the darkness the four hands came together in a strange grip. For a moment it was something grappling and releasing. Then the hands came back to their original positions. Manik was holding the pullover Annie knitted for him and had held in her hand a little while ago. Both of them felt struck by a strange sense of ecstasy.

Both of them continued to walk silently for some time. The orderlies were at some distance ahead of them, Jennie followed them on the *sampani* cart and then behind the cart were Annie and Manik. Each in a joyful bliss.

-"I had seen you knitting this sweater also in the school. I had thought it was for Pincot."

Annie stopped and held both of Manik's hands in her own. She then said, "Had there been light, I needn't have asked this question… But here we are in pitch darkness. I can only feel your presence, not look at the expression on your face. Is this really a simple and natural question or a satire born out of jealousy?"

-"What do you think?" Manik was smiling but Annie couldn't see in the darkness. She left his hands and kept walking.

-"Look, the answer to a question is not another question. Had you not mentioned Pincot's name, I would have treated this as a simple question. Before this also, I had seen jealousy and dislike in your eyes for Pincot."

-"Are you sure what you saw in my eyes was jealousy?"

-"Look, women are seldom wrong in these matters. But let me tell you something else."

-"What?"

-"Okay, leave that aside for now. We shall talk about it some other time. It is quite late now, and you have already come very far. You will have to walk back."

-"Don't worry about me, this is my village. I can walk anywhere anytime in the night also, no matter how late it is. But for now, I must accompany you to the Kothi."

-"Then you have to agree to my request."

-"What?"

-"You must have a cup of tea with me. You know Roopy makes tea. She comes from the upper caste." Annie smiled.

-"That's not the issue. You know very well that both I and Mohan Mani do not practice any untouchability. I accept your request for tea. ... The tea leaves in my house have become stale. Actually, the tea packet is opened only when you visit us. We do not have tea regularly at home. Now tell me what 'something' you wanted to tell me."

-"Oh, you have not forgotten that! To tell you the truth, it just came out of my mouth. Now I feel a bit shy."

-"Shy? Then it must be something important and serious. I must hear what it is about. Then only shall I return peacefully."

-"Fine, then first listen to another serious matter, later we come to that."

-"Go ahead."

-"For some time now, you have been seeing Pincot coming to my house rather frequently and also sometimes he has been walking with me and coming to the school with me."

-"Sure I have seen."

-"That was only to maintain the decorum of a host, just out of courtesy. In stating this now, and I shall explain the word 'now' a little later, I have no hesitation to state that Pincot did have a soft, amorous feeling towards me. But that was all one-sided. In fact, till the day before yesterday, I had not only a dislike for him but also a sort of aversion for him which bordered almost on hatred. He tried a couple of times to flirt with me but I strongly disapproved of his moves and within the limits of being a host, I very much displayed my strong dislike for it. I can say with confidence that after my reaction, there has been a marked change in his attitude not only towards me but life in general which culminated in the event of last night which was certainly miraculous."

-"Miraculous! In what sense?"

-"Just wait, we forgot everything while talking. We have arrived at the gate of the Bungalow, Jennie is shouting and the orderlies are standing by the *sampani* cart. Let's go inside and discuss over a cup of tea."

Manik felt surprised.

Jennie and Manik along with Annie came to her private room. Annie sat with Jennie on the bed and Manik occupied the only chair in the room. Roopy arrived. She was asked to bring three cups of tea. There came suddenly a loud noise from the main dining room. Jennie got up and shut the door. Manik had smelled the strong odour of liquor while entering the Bungalow.

-"Thanks Jennie", Annie remarked with happiness, "You got up to shut the door. I thought you were going as usual to join the party in the main hall."

-"No, see since I became your disciple, I gave up all the old habits. Do you need privacy? In that case, I can go to the hall and check if Pincot has come back."

-"Sit down. If Pincot had arrived he would certainly have come to this room. In any case, when Roopy returns with tea, we can ask her. I don't need privacy. You can very well be here." Annie replied.

-"But you continued talking in private while walking and did not even get into the cart. I thought something more was left to talk about in private. Probably that is the reason Manikji has come along this far at such a late hour."

-"Jennie, you have accepted me as a teacher, like Pincot but unlike him, you have not yet become dispassionate. Your envy is the proof. Actually on the way we had been discussing Pincot and we came here as it remained unfinished. That's why I brought him and offered him a cup of tea, nothing more."

-"It seems you have not yet trusted your disciple. But frankly, I felt like teasing you a little after spending the whole evening in such serious environment."

Roopy had arrived with tea.

Everyone began to sip tea. Roopy remained standing as if expecting further orders.

-"Roopy, any news of Pincot?"

-"No Ma'am. It was under discussion in the main dining hall also. Seeing you getting late, it was my idea to send the orderlies."

-"You? Not Peterson?"

-"I went to remind him."

-"Oh, tomorrow all the guests are leaving. Then Peterson will be under self-control. But Jennie, I shall miss you greatly."

-"Don't worry Annie, I am not going tomorrow with the party. I shall continue staying with you a little longer if you allow me. Only when I prove a perfect disciple, I shall leave for Purnia. I have to learn a lot from you."

-"Oh Jennie, you really took a lot of load off my mind. Thank you so much."

Annie again kissed Jennie out of love. Then she said, "Jennie, suddenly a thought came to my mind like lightning. I want to keep you here near me always. Let me talk to Peterson. If you stay a little longer here, certainly both of you will get a chance to understand each other. As my brother is younger than me and my father is very old and not in a position to move around, it falls upon me to handle everything. I shall have to go to Purnia and convey our request to your father there. At this moment, let us see Manikji off. Manikji, I have a wish."

-"What's that?" Manik had finished his tea by then.

-"You have the sweater on your shoulder. Why don't you give it a try and see if it fits you."

-"But I am going to wear it under my *kurta*."

-"I should anyway see if it is made well or not."

Manik removed his *kurta* and put on the sweater. Annie got up and touched various parts of his body, the neck, the arm, the underarm, the belly etc. and was quite satisfied with her knitting. She then said, "It fits you well, … how do you feel?"

-"It's comfortable and fits well. Thank you very much. But for me, your feeling is more important."

Jennie looked at both of them.

Annie suddenly became grave, and ordering Roopy to take away the cups and dishes, asked her what was the menu for the dinner.

Manik noticed the sudden change in Annie's behaviour but could not immediately understand the reason behind it. And whatever he could guess made him sad. He continued looking at Annie without a blink.

… Aged around thirty … extremely fair, attractive …with large blue eyes….and sexy...

Even though Annie had wrapped herself in a shawl, Manik could easily feel her slender and proportionate body.

Jennie looked at Manik once and then at Annie. Annie had begun making the bed which was already in place.

-"Annie, you didn't tell me about the miraculous transformation of Pincot", Manik asked her suddenly.

-"Oh", Annie was taken aback, then she composed herself, smiled and said, "Pincot's ghost has not left you yet."

-"It's not the ghost Annie, but my worry for the future." By the time Manik had composed himself.

-"The same worry haunts us also. After all, where did he go?" It was about Pincot's disappearance last night.

-"No doubt it is worrisome. Had he gone to Purnia, he should have come back by now. May be he has gone far away to some undisclosed place. Now the only recourse left is to keep searching and waiting. ... Strange ... Anyway, it's getting late. Please take your dinner and I take leave."

Manik got up from the chair, said good bye and left the room.

-"Hold on", Annie shouted, "Let me tell two orderlies to accompany you."

-"No no, there is no need for that. I am not afraid of anything, after all this is my village."

-"Fine, let me walk with you down to the gate."

-"Please leave that, why bother?"

-"But I want to." Annie's words were a kind of order as well as an entreaty.

-"Let me also accompany", Jennie added.

-"No, you arrange the dinner with the help of Roopy in the meantime. I shall be back in no time."

Annie and Manik proceeded towards the gate.

-"You didn't tell", Manik again asked.

-"What?"

-"What I asked."

-"Oh, you haven't yet forgotten that? You are great."

-"How can I forget your words? Tell me is it possible?"

-"You are stubborn. Now it is no use. You must have guessed everything."

-"But certainly I didn't understand anything. It's true."

Manik stopped.

The two orderlies had gone back.

Pushing Manik ahead, Annie said, "Please proceed, it is getting late for you to return."

-"I shall move only after you have told me."

-"Means you will move only on my instructions."

Annie suddenly felt like teasing him. She smiled in the darkness.

Manik misinterpreted the words 'instruction' and 'move' and said with a smile, "You try and see whether I obey you or not".

-"Only time will tell."

-"Surely."

-"But with what authority shall I order you?"

Suddenly Annie became grave. The smile vanished from her lips.

-"Authority?" Manik repeated, "Why? You have all the authority. Don't you think love is supreme?"

Having said so, Manik became grave too and for a moment he was at a loss. He realised that he should not have spoken like he did. And in quick succession, he did something more terrible. He took both of Annie's hands into his own.

Annie was stumped. No one realised what was happening in the impulse of the moment. First time in her life, she did not resist, instead she let her hands go. For a brief moment, both held each other's hands, touching intimately, soothing, fingers of both the hands caressing them involuntarily as if both were hypnotised, none saying a word.

Suddenly Annie pulled her hands and said, "You felt jealous whenever you saw me with Pincot. You know I always enjoyed this feeling of yours. I simply loved it. That's the only thing I wanted to tell you."

And she just turned around, waved good bye and vanished in the darkness without waiting.

Manik was taken aback by the sudden departure of Annie without even coming to the gate or instructing the watchman to open that. However, he could realise Annie's voice had become choked of emotion and she was not in a position to speak.

He kept looking at the female figure walking back in the darkness. He felt as if she was wiping her eyes. Why?

He waited a while for Annie to turn back but to no avail. He quickly walked up to the gate. The watchman opened the gate and he came out.

The gate closed again. Manik again stopped as if he were trying to survey Annie's entire existence in darkness. In his imagination he saw Annie crossing the hall, going to her bedroom, he could see the cot, the bed, the bedsheet, the pillow cover, the chair, the table, papers, all the items there in vivid detail.

He tried to figure out why Annie's voice became choked while describing her pleasure at Manik's jealousy towards Pincot. Why did she become emotional? Why could she not see him off as usual by taking him the outside the gate? So many questions but no answer.

Whatever Manik could think made him sad. He felt pity for Annie and a sense of frustration for himself. He looked at the already shut-down Williams Market with vacant eyes and slowly walked towards his house.

He had seen Annie for the first time at the Bungalow when she had invited him along with Mohan Mani to discuss about the school. That was some four years ago. Before that, he had heard that the daughter and son of William Kutt, who had been studying in Calcutta, had returned as Kutt had grown old. His son Peterson was to take charge of the Estate and all financial matters. His daughter would look after him. He heard several stories about the brother-sister duo. He was told that Peterson was very hot-headed and impulsive, and he used to always scold the accountant, orderlies, butler and other servants. However, people said that the daughter was very soft-spoken and she hardly spoke at all. She was just the opposite of her brother and spent her time mostly reading books. She would sometimes visit Williams Bazaar, she was beautiful and attractive etc.

She had introduced herself during that meeting, without waiting for her father or brother to say anything. A woman in her early twenties, extremely fair as the British should be, lean and tall but healthy and well-built, wearing a blouse and a skirt.

After the school began to function, albeit with very few children, she came to visit once in the afternoon. During that period Manik was the acting Headmaster. Pandit Trilochan Jha

Shastri had not yet retired from Purnia Zila School. Her first visit to the school had become the talk of the town in entire Dharampur village.

Annie came to school the next day also. She made it a regular habit to go to the school, inquire about the school affairs during her short stay and then return.

Within a week she proposed to Manik about teaching English to students. Mohan Mani, who had been teaching English, had to go on an errand concerning the Independence Movement for a few days. Hence teaching English was a problem. Annie's proposal was welcomed by all. Everyone was pleased.

Annie now became a regular teacher at the school. Manik came to know her more intimately.

During these interactions, Manik learnt that Annie had been in regular contact with the Royal Asiatic Society. She had studied a lot of writings of Sir William Jones, Colebrook and Max Muller. As she studied them, she became more and more interested in India, Indian knowledge systems, Indian traditions and customs, Indian literature, philosophy and science. As she learnt about the subjects, she became more interested in further studies. She wanted to study Indian philosophy and do social service here.

These two, the study of Indian philosophy and social service, became her goal in life. She did not want to waste her life by getting married and having a family and children like any typical European woman or more so like a typical Indian woman. ... Although the scope of social service in India was very wide and one could pick up any direction, she thought to concentrate on education, particularly female education in a rural area which was almost non-existent. "I should stay in this village where my father has landed property. This village is totally undeveloped. Although my father wants me to settle in Calcutta and get married, I have decided against that as it will not help me fulfil my dreams. I am in favour of Indian Independence and I was happy at the demand of Independence last year at the Lahore Congress by Jawahar Lal Nehru. I was thrilled when an Indian flag was hoisted on the 26th of January. This event had been appreciated by only a handful of Europeans, most others detested it... Whatever I shall do in future is a separate matter. For the present, I consider education as the path to liberation of the masses and also the path to Independence. So I shall continue to work in this field." She had told Manik in her chats.

Annie began her school routine on a daily basis. She was very regular and would not tolerate being late on any account. Manik and Annie interacted more and more, came to know each other more and more and with every interaction, an appreciation for each other kept growing. The growing interaction led to liking for each other. Manik's faith and devotion to Annie also grew every day.

But he could not make out what Annie had told him a few minutes before. Whatever he could relate to made him more distraught... a feeling of regret, something inexplicable.

He had reached his house. On the *dalan*, his father lay awake. "Who is there?" the old man asked.

-"Manik", he replied.

-"Go and have your dinner. It's quite late now."

On the veranda, the oil lamp was burning. There was a sheet spread on the cot meant for Manik. After his wife's death, he had made it a practice to sleep on the *dalan* and not inside. He had been pressurised both by the family members and the society to get married again but he had decided against it. He remained firm and devoted time to the Independence Movement which had been gaining momentum every passing day.

And then came the school, and Annie. The intimacy between them slowly kept increasing.

The Morning of Ninth August 1942

Annie was aroused by a violent shaking Jennie gave her.

-"What's the matter, Jennie?" Annie sat on the bed.

A mixed and unclear noise was coming from Williams Market through the window. The servants within the Kothi were running here and there, not able to understand what had been going on outside.

Roopy entered the room with two cups of tea, with a confused smile, and said, "I have been checking frequently whether Ma'am has left the bed. You are late today. There is some commotion outside the gate, around the market area. It seems Manik Babu had come very early in the morning and instructed the watchman at the gate to keep the gate always closed and not open it for anyone. He left quickly for the market area. It is not clear what is happening outside but within the Bungalow everyone is restive."

In fact, Roopy had not been able to guess the goings-on outside. She had got only some hints from Ramy but no details.

Jennie was no different. She had sensed some trouble as her Mother and other children had arrived in the Bungalow during the night from Purnia. They had told her about the possibility of large-scale violence and disruptions and finding the Kothi at Dharampur rather safe, they had come to take shelter here. Some more British had also arrived.

Taking care of the guests was now the responsibility of Jennie. She was the de facto owner and Lady of the Kothi after her marriage with Peterson. The marriage had been solemnised in a church in Calcutta.

Unfortunately, Mr. William Kutt had not been witness to this marriage. He had died a few years before.

Annie came back from the bathroom and taking the tea cup from Roopy sat on the bed. She told Roopy, "The tea has become cold. Take the cups and fetch another two cups of hot tea." Roopy ran towards the kitchen.

-"What has happened, Jennie?" Annie inquired, "Have the guests taken tea?"

-"All the guests had tea. Everyone is scared and sitting huddled in the main drawing room."

-"Why?"

-"There is a commotion outside. There has been some sabotage in Williams Market. Thank God Manikji arrived in the nick of time and hooliganism stopped. ... That's what we got to know. It seems when Bahadur opened the gate in the morning, as usual, a crowd entered the premises and tore off the British flag flying atop. Manikji entered just at that time and drove the crowd away, instructed Bahadur not to open the gate at all and left. There was no incidence of violence at all. That's what the orderlies have told us. I must profusely thank your Manikji." Saying this she shook Annie's chin in a loving gesture.

-"Why do you say 'your Manikji'?"

-"Yes, I am right."

-"What right? Have you observed anything between us?"

-"Almost always, particularly over the last few years, I have been watching..."

-"Can you describe what has been your observation?"

-"Visible attraction for each other, a sea of affinity and sky-high tenderness."

-"Oh Jennie, you almost caught me. Don't you find a similar attraction, affinity and tenderness in me for you?"

-"See Annie, you can lecture me for long hours on Indian philosophy, literature and traditions, I shall accept all that. But as far as the distinction in relation to the attraction between two women and that between a man and a woman is concerned, you cannot claim to have superior wisdom. On the contrary, my sixth sense in this matter is far superior than you may admit."

-"No doubt, you are quite clever, that is proved beyond doubt by the way you managed to trap my brother into matrimony. Not only that, you have gained complete control over him, that's much more surprising and tells volumes about your astuteness."

Having thus teased her sister-in-law, Annie pulled her close, gave her a tight embrace till Roopy entered the room with tea.

They separated from each other and turned to tea.

-"Look Jennie", Annie spoke with a tone of gravity in her voice, "India is totally different from Europe. In Europe, it is common to get into marital relations between a French and a British, an Italian and a German or a Spaniard and a French etc. Even we easily get into marital relations with Greeks and Americans. But here it is not so. Here the society is divided into castes, sub-castes and the like. Even within a caste matrimony is not approved easily between two persons without looking into their genealogy. Marriage outside a caste is strictly forbidden. You can say that India is very conservative and even dogmatic in this matter. But looked from another angle you will find that it is very tolerant, generous and noble."

-"Means what?"

-"See, India is divided into many religions, a number of sects within the same religion, and different faiths. So much so that it is not uncommon to find persons within the same family following different sects or faiths. Still, there is harmony among all. People practise co-existence. In that sense, the level of individual freedom and consciousness found in India is unique and cannot be found elsewhere in the world. No matter if various religious entities or faiths have debated at the intellectual level or not, in the end, there has been always a tolerant attitude towards all. You don't find a religious war having taken place here in its entire history. Even invaders, practising religions external to this land and with antagonistic views, became a natural part of the society and have lived in harmony. That's the greatest secret of unity in diversity in India."

-"Really India is a unique country."

-"One more unique tradition about India will surprise you."

-"What's that?"

-"See, in Europe, first a boy meets a girl, they begin dating each other for some time, personal interaction increases understanding of each other and finally they marry. That marriage, the so-called love marriage, frequently breaks up leading to divorce. Here in India, only the Muslim community has the provision of divorce, which in any case is not part of the original Indian culture. The Hindu society is totally different. Here a boy and a girl, complete strangers to each other, get married as arranged by their parents. Love develops after marriage and that makes a permanent bond. Divorce is practically unheard of in Indian society, particularly among the upper castes. The marriage is guided by the sense of duty to each other's families and regard for each other which is the backbone of the society."

-"Annie, you mentioned upper castes. Does that mean the traditions in lower castes are different?"

-"Yes, to an extent that is so. Among lower castes, although divorce per se is not practised, there is the practice of polygamy and also widow marriage. Although the practice of polygamy existed among upper castes also in the Middle Ages, this is being discouraged now and the instances are reducing considerably. I can foretell that this will be completely abolished in the near future but there is no practice of widow marriage yet among the upper castes."

-"I am surprised how you learnt so much about India. Was it from books only?"

-"Certainly not only from books." Annie smiled.

-"Then?"

-"Talking to people. Especially with Manikji."

-"With Manikji? And you never discussed your own marriage?" Jennie was astonished.

-"The question does not arise. Just now I mentioned to you about the marriage-related customs in Indian society. ... You must realise this is not only difficult but almost impossible here. Both I and Manikji know this very well."

-"So are you going to remain unmarried all your life? Manikji at least had been married, although his wife died, that's a different matter."

-"As far as I know, Manikji may have got married at an early age. As his age is also advanced, most likely he is not going to get married again. As far as I am concerned, I decided long ago to remain unmarried, and on top of it I am now close to forty."

There was an interruption.

Roopy came and informed them that they were required to be in the main drawing room.

Both of them realised there were guests in the house. Jennie left the room feeling sad and Annie began getting ready in an absentminded state.

When Annie arrived in the main drawing room in that absentminded state, everyone was startled: the middle-aged wife of the Collector of Purnia, her two young daughters, a growing up son, an Indigo-farmer friend of Peterson and his entire family, who had arrived to save themselves from the ongoing troubles of the year Nineteen Hundred Forty-two, Peterson himself and his two friends from Calcutta who had come for a hunting expedition and the rank and file of the assembled servants, so much so that for an instant even Jennie could not control her amazement.

Only Roopy was calm, she had accompanied her Ma'am after Annie was ready. It was she who had applied on Annie's shining white forehead a red circular dot of vermillion. She was quietly smiling and observing the reaction of the guests while looking at Ma'am with a side glance at intervals.

Amazement was written on the face of each and every person present there. This was partly because of Annie's beauty past her youth accentuated by the Indian attire consisting of a sari and a blouse, her attractive features and her dignified persona. But the most important reason for amazement was the red dot on her forehead which had completely changed her familiar appearance.

Annie's personality had undergone a change in the recent past with her wearing the handmade cotton saris. This had been known to some of the guests present there. Some also knew about her passion for the spinning wheel, Charkha, and its regular use. But the red dot on the forehead was completely unexpected and new to all.

Along with other guests, both Jennie and Peterson were also dismayed at the unexpected makeup Annie wore. There were diverse reactions.

As the guests were talking in English, Roopy was unable to understand all, but she could comprehend the gestures which were all-round praise for Annie, particularly by the ladies. Most of the gentlemen showed some dissatisfaction, some distaste, and some were just neutral.

-"Roopy, bring coffee for all", Annie ordered.

Roopy vanished immedaitely.

The Indigo farmer friend of Peterson commented with some dissatisfaction on the use of Sari and Vermillion, "Mr. Peterson, there is a revolutionary in your house." Then turning towards Annie, he continued, "Miss Annie, I hope we don't have to worry about your being a revolutionary. I have come to know that your Gandhi has ordered people of the entire country to resort to violence against the British. The entire British India is in the grip of terror because of that order. We have taken shelter here considering this to be a safe place."

Peterson kept quiet. When he had seen the Charkha for the first time some years ago in Annie's possession, he had angrily opposed it and had spoken a lot against it in disgust. But his opposition had no effect on his elder sister. He in fact was defeated in the end by Annie's persuasive arguments. This happened just two years after their father's death.

Just the next year, Annie had begun wearing the hand-woven Indian sari. Peterson had become annoyed that day also. Whosoever among the British saw her was also upset and annoyed. Prominent among them were the Collectors of Purnia and Bhagalpur and several other officials. But everyone felt defeated at the arguments Annie put forth. No one could persuade her to give up the Indian ways of living.

But Annie never felt defeated in her life. Whatever she desired and whenever she wanted, she did things according to her wishes. Looking at it from that angle, she remained the winner all the time. To the Indigo farmer guest she replied, "Dear John uncle, you are like my father. Expressing my deepest regard to you, I assure you that you are totally safe here. You just mentioned that I am a revolutionary. Let me explain: the rise of Manchester has been solely due to the Indian cotton. Before you brought Manchester clothes here, Indian men and women were wearing handmade clothes, also called Khadi clothes, like what I am wearing today. After 1905 many Indians went back to wearing Khadi, prominent among them being the revolutionaries of Bengal. But let me also stress that all those who wear Khadi are not revolutionaries. It's a different matter that all such people love their country; call themselves patriots and in some manner or other are connected with the Independence Movement of Gandhiji. It is also true that there are several others who are equally genuine patriots but do not always use Khadi."

Everyone was listening with rapt attention.

Pausing for an instant, Annie continued, "I have great regard for Mahatma Gandhi. That is the reason for my wearing Khadi and also using the Charkha. You may consider this as my disloyalty. If any of my behaviour, speech or action has hurt you in any manner, I request you to condone me, as it is not my intention at all to hurt anyone in any manner. I shall consider myself fortunate to receive your forgiveness."

Everyone had mellowed by the time Annie spoke her last words. Her politeness and decency had won over all of them, so much so that the women present there had tears in their eyes.

Again pausing for an instant and before anyone could say anything on what she said, she looked at Mr. Johnson and said, "Dear John Uncle, certainly none of you here has to fear any danger from me but ... one point..."

-"What?" Everyone exclaimed in chorus, with Mr. Johnson's voice being the loudest.

-"All of you are prisoners here." Annie smilingly stated.

-"Prisoner? Whose prisoner?" Suddenly all of them turned pale with fear and astonishment. They started to guess what Annie had plotted against them as she was loyal to Gandhiji and was very much part of the Indian movement.

Annie looked at the drained faces, smiled a little and declared, "You all are prisoners of Indianness..."

-"What is that?" Again a chorus voice rose from all sides.

-"Simple: You all are my prisoner. Dear John Uncle, you have been in India for a long time. You must have known about the Indian way of treating their guests."

-"Sure I do. I know here even the poorest among the poor treats the guests the best as if Gods had descended at his door.

They feed you so well with so many varieties of food that you cannot but praise them."

-"That's right, but you still do not know an important part of the tradition. People hide and keep in safe custody an important item of the guest, so that they prolong their stay searching the lost item and spend some more time with the host. That way they become a prisoner of affection. You all will be a prisoner in this Bungalow and not allowed to go out at all till all is quiet. And you all know a prisoner has to endure a lot of hardship. So again, please pardon me for all those hardships you will face while being a captive here in this Bungalow."

Everyone was relieved and clapped in excitement. They thanked Annie profusely for her hospitality.

After a long time, Peterson felt proud of his elder sister's behaviour. He had never liked the Charkha, the Khadi cotton saris and dresses, Annie's commitment to the school, her devotion towards the Indian culture and traditions etc. He always felt humiliated even during his father's time and certainly in later years as well.

Roopy brought coffee for all. The bearer came to ask for the choice of breakfast for the guests and left the hall with orders. People changed the topic of discussion during coffee.

-"The names of Mohan Mani and Manik Jha are known to people as far as my Raniganj. I am told these two names are quite well-known even in Bhagalpur. I hear that it was Manik who came in the morning and stopped people from doing any damage here. He just allowed them to snatch and throw the British flag. ... Is he not a revolutionary?" Mr. Johnson asked Peterson.

-"John Uncle", Peterson replied with some disgust, "Every Swaraji (freedom fighter) here is a revolutionary. No one wants the presence of the British here. But this Manik Jha is slightly different. Today also, just because he arrived a little late the flag had been torn and thrown. Everyone retreated on his command and went out of the campus. Everyone obeys his orders."

-"Is he not a revolutionary like other freedom fighters? I heard that he too is a teacher in your school." Mr. Johnson asked Annie.

-"No, Uncle John, he had a soft corner for the revolutionaries to begin with but with time he, like Mohan Mani, became a devotee of Gandhiji and has become a follower of Gandhi's Satyagraha, non-cooperation, self-reliance, and non-violence. He is leading the Quit India movement launched by Gandhiji in this region. Mohan Mani, who is comparatively more mature and elderly and undisputed leader of all, has gone to the District Headquarters at Bhagalpur to plan for the success of the movement."

-"I see. Mohan Mani's name as a freedom fighter is also quite famous and people refer to him with great respect. I think because of the Gandhian principles, Manik Jha did not allow hooliganism and violence here within the Bungalow. Thank him and you all that we are safe here."

While Mr. Johnson was still speaking, suddenly there was an interruption. Munshi came running from Williams Market. "The market is now quite peaceful, thanks to Manikji. There was not much destruction either. Manikji prevented people from looting the shops. But the crowd managed to take down the flag from my office and burnt that, they also celebrated burning the flag" He said betraying his happiness. None other than Annie, not even Jennie, noticed the Munsi's glowing face.

Everyone, including Peterson, became glum hearing about the burning of the flag.

Munsi went near Annie and lowering his voice told her, "There is a message for you from Manikji."

Everyone became alert.

-"What is the message?"

-"There is a meeting at 3 p.m. at the school. Manikji told me to inform you."

-"Fine, get the breakfast ready for the guests quickly." She ordered the bearer. Munsi left.

-"Will you go?" Peterson asked with a little worry on his face. He has great affection for his sister but is equally afraid of her. He knows Annie's decisions can't be changed. Any attempt to oppose her is not only difficult, it's impossible.

-"Shall have to go, after all the meeting is at the school."

Peterson became somewhat grave and restless hearing her reply. He knew how she reacted.

-"Under such volatile circumstances?" Purnia Collector's wife questioned, "Among those revolutionaries?"

Annie smiled and said, "There is nothing to fear."

"My sister is respected like Mother Mary here", Peterson added with a touch of sarcasm.

One of the two friends of Peterson, who had arrived from Calcutta, whispered to the other, "Has Annie, as a maiden, given birth to a child like Mother Mary?"

-"Is that the sole reason Mother Mary is respected in Europe? Idiot... Has Annie's dignity, compassion, dedication and affection to all not touched you at all? Strange! Really you will never become a sensible person and will remain a stupid as ever. Even though born to European parents, Annie is not European by nature, she has always belonged to India, she is cent-per-cent Indian and you should know that in India there is no scope for a child out of wedlock, particularly among the upper strata of society having rigid customs."

Whispering stopped.

-"Is Annie respected here for these qualities?"

-"Certainly. ... But I also have a small contribution in that." Peterson smiled and looking at Annie told the assembly, "She became respectable because of her services to the school, but on her insistence, I agreed to give homestead land rights to Jolaha tribe and some other landless people in the village. This has increased esteem for her in the eyes of everyone here."

-"But you have done a very objectionable work." Mr. Johnson was prompt to point out.

-"What?"

-"By promoting the local Jolahas you have greatly harmed Manchester."

-"If you think carefully John Uncle, I have not done much harm. Even now the majority of Indians use clothes from Manchester which are much superior and cheaper. Khadi is comparatively expensive. Only freedom fighters and the followers of Gandhiji use it. Here in this village, a limited number of people in the upper strata of the society wear Khadi because of the influence of Mohan Mani and Manik Jha."

The discussion was abruptly stopped as the bearer announced breakfast service.

Bottles began to be opened at the breakfast table. Everyone was engaged.

Annie returned to her room after the breakfast.

-"Gandhi's Quit India Movement is utter nonsense." Mr. Johnson quipped, "This will be soon suppressed with an iron hand. I have talked to both the Collectors of Purnia and Bhagalpur. The British Army at Calcutta, Bombay, Madras and even Danapur Cantt. have been kept ready."

Just then Peterson's friend Jim, who had arrived from Calcutta, commented, "How long will these half-naked half-starved unarmed people, who cherished tearing a flag, sustain against the British Army? They will be driven away or killed in no time. British Prime Minister Churchill has an elaborate plan for suppressing the movement. He is dead against the demand for freedom by Indians. He has very clearly stated that such a demand is preposterous. Indians simply don't have the capacity to rule. They are used to being slaves for ages."

-"Absolutely", Mr. Johnson added with emphasis, "You all will see, the movement will be crushed and people will be butchered in the same way as it happened at Jallianwala Bagh."

- "But remember one point", Peterson's other friend from Calcutta, Nelson, who was more sensible and grave, commented in a measured voice, "I came to know from very reliable sources at Calcutta that after the World War, condition is not very good in England. The economy is in tatters. The situation is really grave. The second point to note is that Gandhi was very successful in his movement in Africa. He was very much respected there and he is the person leading the movement here too. He is something like a wizard. So we should not judge the fate of the present movement so quickly."

-"Nelson Junior", Mr. Johnson was now excited in his response, "Whatever may be the reason, do you think there will ever be a sunset on the British Empire? Never. I doubt if you also, like Annie, are nurturing a silent idea of treason."

-"John Uncle", Nelson Junior protested sharply, "I strongly object to your statement. If you wish, you can withdraw your statement like a gentleman. ... I am of the opinion that no one, from any country, can be a traitor. Everyone loves his or her motherland. I also love England and so does Annie, for sure. The only difference is that while I am mesmerized by India being a strange land, Annie has been attracted to the Indian culture, its ancient knowledge and literature and she has devoted her services to the society here. To serve is part of her character, here she is serving the local community, if she were in London, she would have served the society there as well. This feature is reflected in Annie's feminine and motherly instincts. May I ask you a question – we do revere the Greek culture and civilization.

Does that mean we are traitors, supporting Greeks against England? No, never."

Nelson Junior's arguments were so forceful that the listeners found themselves in total agreement. None would utter a word. Everyone appreciated the depth of his reasoning. The breakfast had almost come to an end, although bottles were still being opened and drinks were going on.

The Indigo farmer of Raniganj had taken a few too many drinks and was now almost stoned. He got excited and retorted, "Mr. Nelson Junior, your statements are partly correct and factual but the way you labelled me as uncivilised in the very beginning of your statement has hurt me greatly. This is against courtesy. If you wish, you can seek an apology."

-"John Uncle, if anything I said have unknowingly hurt you or anyone here, I do apologize."

Suddenly the discussion was interrupted by a messenger from the Collector of Purnia, who came riding a horse and declared that the rebellion had been crushed and Purnia was now completely peaceful.

Everyone felt relieved. Especially Jennie's mother, brother, sister and Peterson heaved a sigh of relief. Peterson said, "Thanks, this is what we expected. I agree John Uncle, we the English are a great race. They possess not only the military strength and wisdom but also the qualities of deception. These three qualities are essential to run a vast empire like this. You know, I have done an important work recently."

-"What's that?" Mr. Johnson was very inquisitive.

-"You know well that using the tricks of wit, deception and force, my father had acquired the large tracts of land belonging to the Muslim Zamindar Haji Hazrat Jafar Ali. Mr. Ali was a lazy and lustful person. He had a large number of wives and concubines in his harem. People in his family became traitors and the economic condition worsened day by day. That's the reason my father could make suitable moves and acquire his land. But that created another problem: the entire Muslim community here became angry with the British and there was an outrage against our family."

-"Then?"

-"Then Father thought of a plan to assuage their feelings. After some months had passed, he gave generous grants for constructing a Masjid and a Madarsa in the Muslim neighbourhood. People slowly became our friends. ... Later Father also tried to sow seeds of discord between the Hindu and Muslim society. He educated the Muslims about the Muslim League and its principles. That created a feeling of hatred among Muslims towards Hindus. Thus the society remains badly divided."

-"Exactly similar things I have also done in my area."

-"More recently I have done something more."

-"What's that?"

-"You know that Mauza Dharampur is a very big *Panchayat*. There are Muslim Tolas both in the eastern and western parts of the village. In the West, there are two large Tolas of Muslims by the side of the Muslim Tola of Dharampur. I conspired with them and suggested that they should form a separate Panchayat exclusively for Muslims. I suggested that they should appeal to the Collector of Bhagalpur. Separately I talked to the Collector of Bhagalpur to consider the demand of Muslims for a separate Panchayat sympathetically. The Muslim leaders met the Collector and their proposal was accepted. In the near future, there will be a new Panchayat exclusively for Muslims there.

-"Wah! Peterson, you did a great job. It was the great Machiavellian strategy. This will be very useful in future. And what about the Muslim Tola in the east?"

-"Actually the Hindus too have large populations there."

-"But who has the majority?"

-"Muslims."

-"Fine. That portion falls within the jurisdiction of the Collector of Purnia."

-"Of course."

-"Very good. You should meet the Collector of Purnia and request him to get that part separated from Bhagalpur for the sake of easier administration. It will still be within the control of your Zamindari but they will be divided on religious lines which will be beneficial for us in future."

-"That's fine, but the problem is that the Hindus there will certainly oppose, as some of their land and relations also reside in that part."

-"So what?"

-"There may be a revolt."

-"The British Empire has the means and wisdom to suppress any revolt anywhere within India. That's the reason it is said that **the Sun never sets on the British Empire**. You first meet the Collector of Purnia with your proposal."

Peterson got the hint. He found Mr. John's proposal practical and useful.

-"You do one more thing", Thinking something Mr. Johnson said again, "I guess the population of untouchable castes here is also substantial."

-"Yes it is, but what's with that?"

-"Try brainwashing them so that they begin to hate the upper caste people. You can begin by giving them some special facilities so they become sympathetic towards you. Then you should try..."

-"An initiative in that direction has already been made by giving homestead land rights to Jolahas."

-"This is no doubt very good. You should do similar things for other untouchable castes. Then your efforts will bring results."

-"But what will that lead to?"

-"It will lead to several important developments in the local society and it will have far-reaching consequences on a pan-India level. First and foremost, this will lead to division within the society and the society will become weak. The weaker the Indian society, the better for us to rule them."

Peterson felt a sense of revealation. Mr. Johnson had been thinking very far into the future. The meaning of everything suddenly dawned upon him. He said, "John Uncle, you are great. Your foresight is truly remarkable. I am greatly obliged."

-"Great is the British race which is famous for its foresight. This is the reason that even though French, Dutch and Portuguese all came to India, none could establish their foothold. Those were driven out by us. Now there is the British Empire so large that the Sun never sets on its soil."

Mr. Johnson lifted his glass after this statement. Peterson began thinking hard over the entire discussion.

*

When Jennie entered Annie's room she found her lying on her bed and looking at the ceiling.

-"Are you trying to sleep?"

-"No no, ..." Annie turned around and moved a little on the bed to make space for Jennie to sit.

-"If you were not trying to sleep, certainly you have been thinking about some important problem." Jennie sat by her side on the bed and began stroking her hair.

-"In fact, I am not even thinking anything specific. Rather, I was waiting for you."

-"If not specific, something mundane. Most likely about the school."

-"It is true I keep thinking about the school but presently your guess is far from true."

-"Then you must have been thinking about Manikji or mentally roaming with him."

-"You always imagine Manikji with me", Annie lovingly pulled the chin of her sister-in-law and said, "Today it was Manikji, I think, who saved Williams Market from destruction. Otherwise, the violent crowd could have done anything."

- "You are the sole reason for that, not your brother Peterson. It is because of the affection Manikji has for you. That brought him here to save the property of the Estate. ... But tell me why were you waiting for me? Then I shall also tell you something."

-"I was just longing for you to have coffee together. Are all the guests taken care of well? Your brother and sisters? Are they comfortable?"

-"Everyone is busy with own affairs. There are plenty of drinks and eats. My mother and sisters are taking rest."

-"You didn't give them company in drinking?"

-"I hardly enjoy drinks now. Just one or two, occasionally, I would say. That's all.... In fact, I love your company much more now. That's why I returned back quickly after making all the arrangements for them."

-"To me or to my brother Peterson?"

-"Both", Jennie smiled and going near the gate called Roopy.

Roopy appeared immediately as if she had been waiting just at the door. She was given the orders for coffee. She left.

-"Now tell me what you wanted to tell." Annie asked.

-"Leave that aside, we have talked several times, and you know it so well."

-"What?"

-"Manikji's affection for you is not one-sided."

-"What do you mean?"

-"Look, my dear sis, don't try to be smart. You know very well what I mean to say. If you want to hear it explicitly, which obviously will be pleasing to your ears and will give you a tickling sensation, then let me clearly state that as Manikji has affection for you, so you also have similar affection for him."

-"How do you know?" Annie smiled and asked.

-"I just know, that's it", Jennie lovingly touched Annie's chin and continued, "We may continue with this conversation as long as it pleases you. ... but nothing escapes a woman's sharp eyes. Women have got uncanny abilities to sense love that men don't have. ... I have found it on a number of occasions from your utterances and behaviours. .. Fine, tell me something."

-"What?" Annie looked in anticipation with a smile.

-"Manikji's wife died at a very young age. Even then he did not marry again in spite of the pressure from his parents and the society all around.

-"I really don't know."

-"You two have been in touch with each other now for more than a decade. Still, you say 'I don't know', but I know."

-"You know? How? Strange." Annie looked at her inquisitively.

-"You told me long ago because of your commitment to the society and also because of lack of a suitable match, you decided to remain unmarried. That's true, isn't it?"

-"That's right." Annie looked at Jennie with surprise. Slowly she began reflecting. She never thought the way Jennie put it. Whereas she had been thinking of so many aspects of Manik's life for so many years, she never imagined such things. It was strange that Jennie, whom she considered lazy and dull-headed, and who of course managed a whimsical man like Peterson and kept herself busy with domestic affairs, could think that far. Has she got a sharper mind and a sharp eye than she (Annie) thought?

Looking Annie indifferent, Jennie added further, "Is it now clear just because you decided not to marry, Manikji also decided not to marry? Look, this is the climax of pure love, where sacrifice for each other is the measure of the depth of devotion. Manikji's sacrifice is purely for your sake."

Annie didn't allow Jennie to elaborate further. She just embraced her tightly. It felt they shared pleasure.

Annie felt as if an overcast sky had suddenly cleared and a bright sun was shining all around in which Manikji's benign countenance was brilliantly lit. That face had ocean-like gravity, strong willpower, and unbreakable resolve. The eyes radiated with a fountain of empathy and affection flowed with unwavering brilliance.

Suddenly she was filled with a strange void, so much so that she could not release Jennie from her embrace.

Roopy entered with coffee. The two women separated and took their cups.

Jennie looked at Annie and sensed her sadness. She tried to change the subject and said, "I want to learn to wear a sari from Roopy. ... and today I plan to go with you in a sari."

Even in her sadness, Annie smiled and replied, "Today only you begin to learn to wear a sari and then also come with me in a sari!"

-"Yes."

-"It will be a scandal." Annie laughed loudly.

-"What's the problem?"

-"You know it takes a long practice to master wearing a sari. Have you not noticed how many days I had to ask Roopy to teach me the art? Without practice if you go walking with me, there will be a scandalous scene created on the road, you somewhere and your sari somewhere else. Imagine what will happen then?"

Roopy also laughed at this description as she could figure out what was being talked about.

-"There is another problem."

-"What's that?"

-"Peterson does not like it. He has somehow allowed me as I am older to him, he knows I do not listen to him but he will be very angry with you for sure."

-"Don't worry about him. I shall handle his anger and manage to convince him."

-"I know you are an expert in handling men. That's how you managed so many men in the past and now you are deftly managing my brother."

-"Whatever that may be", Jennie lovingly pulled the chin of her sister-in-law and added, "Certainly, it was my quality of managing men that you went to my parents asking their consent for marriage with your brother."

-"Not only for my brother, for myself also. I saw your talent. Where could I find such a nice sister-in-law, a close friend and a confidant? It was my selfishness too."

- "Do you want to go with me today?"

-"Yes, I want to go and rest assured, I shall not interfere in any private talk between you and Manikji. I shall keep distance whenever needed."

-"You know very well there is nothing private between me and Manikji and there is no chance of it even in future either. But even if there is something, how can that remain hidden from your prying eyes? You only mentioned the women's insight just now. ... Should I tell you something?"

-"What?"

-"I was greatly surprised when you mentioned a woman's insight."

-"Why? What was so strange about it?"

-"So far I had considered you a happy-go-lucky bimbo busy with her daily affairs. But you surprised me with your feminine insight and the way you logically analysed why Manikji promised to remain unmarried after his wife's death. I never paid attention to these matters. You have turned out to be really sharp."

Jennie was smiling while listening to Annie's statements. She added, "Yes, your surprise is natural."

-"Why natural?"

-"A woman is in general inward looking. You are the opposite – outward-looking, like men. That's why you are not able to pay attention to fine details about a woman's sensibilities and insights. There can be a number of other reasons also but in my opinion, your commitment to social service and attraction towards ancient Indian literature and culture also does not permit you to look into details women see. Now it's too late for you to learn."

-"Why? You are really special, who can analyse events so seriously and logically. Why do you feel it will not be possible in future?"

-"Because for one, you are past your prime to develop the faculties. The time for analysing feminine sensibilities and emotions is either gone or will soon pass. The second is your decision to not get married and a possible third is also the local climate.... but leave them aside. Tell me whether I can accompany you to the school this afternoon. I may go in my usual dress and not in an Indian sari."

-"Listen, Jennie, try to understand. I have taken you to the school, to Manikji's house and also to the village. It was all during a normal situation. But now after the call of Gandhi's Quit India movement, the situation has changed. Especially today, there will be many people from all the Tolas, all of them filled with hatred for the British. No one can predict how they will behave. It may be unsafe for you. I don't feel comfortable taking you along."

-"But that question of security holds for you also."

-"It's different with me. People know my intention towards the local population, their social customs and traditions is very accommodative. They respect me for my work as well as my opinions. In fact that has led to much gossip here about me. You must have noticed that on a number of occasions when we have toured the village together. That's why there is no question about my security at all: I am safe."

-"Fine, if you so wish, I shall not go. But all of us, especially me, will be worried till you return safely. So I suggest apart from the *sampani* cart driver and the attendant, take a few musclemen along as well."

-"Not needed at all. Even *sampani* will be required only during the return journey as it will be dark by that time. No need to worry. You know so many British came to India ... and quite a few of them have been killed also for different reasons. If anything happens .... think on that line." Annie smiled.

-"Nonsense." Jennie pretended to show her displeasure and left the room.

Even though Annie called her back, she did not return. Annie felt greater respect and affection for her sister-in-law.

*

It was already dark when the meeting at the school ended. The school ground was almost full to capacity. A lot of people from several neighbouring villages had come to listen to their popular leader Manik Jha. Everyone knew that Mohan Maniji had gone to Bhagalpur to make this Gandhiji's Quit India movement a great success everywhere.

These two Congress leaders were highly respected in the villages around Dharampur. People had gathered in the meeting with lots of enthusiasm and expectation. Now there will be an end to the atrocities committed by the British. They will be forced to go back to their country and we shall rule our country ourselves. There will be prosperity all around. Rivers of milk and curd will flow in the country. No one will remain poor and hungry. No one will commit any atrocity on any person. That was the hope which had brought so many people to the meeting.

But there were notable absentees too – a large section of Muslims from the two Muslim Tolas had not come to the meeting. They have been trying for the last two years, i.e., since Nineteen hundred Forty, to create a separate Panchayat for Muslims. For this purpose, they have been making frequent trips to Purnia to meet the Collector there. Even then some seven to ten people did arrive from those Tolas. These people have been working with Mohan Mani and Manik Jha for long. They also shouted slogans in praise of Mahatma Gandhi and Jawahar Lal Nehru, like 'Long live Mahatma Gandhi', 'Long live Jawahar Lal Nehru', 'Bharat Mata ki Jai' and 'Inquilab Zindabad' vociferrously along with the rest.

Also among the notable absentees were three teachers of the school – the old Headmaster Pt. Trilochan Jha Shastri, who has retired from this school and was not in good health, and the two newly appointed teachers. The school has now been taken over by the District Board headed by the Collector of Purnia. The two new teachers feared losing their jobs.

Apart from being the founder of the school, Annie has been a regular but honorary teacher of the school from the beginning. Manik has also been an honorary teacher from the beginning but lately, he gave up teaching because of his heavy commitment towards the work of the Congress Party and the Independence Movement. Still, he continues to supervise the operations of the school.

He continued to do this because of Annie. They had quarrelled also. Annie was of the opinion that working as a volunteer, there is no scope for disobedience. But Manik has disagreed as he is an ardent follower of Mahatma Gandhi and his school of thought.

Manik explained in detail the views of Mahatma Gandhi about Truth, Non-violence, and the 'Quit India' movement to the assembled crowd. Describing the contribution of the Congress Party to the Independence Movement, he outlined the historical facts about the entry of the Dutch, the Portuguese and the French via sea route after the land route had been closed by Turkey. The last of the Europeans to land in India were the British under the garb of East India Company, but after the battle of Plassey and Buxar, they became more visible and powerful. They began driving away other Europeans and also started committing atrocities on the local population in order to terrorize them. He explained the first large-scale opposition to British rule during 1857 after which the British East India Company was superseded by the British Crown, direct rule by the British Government, the transition of the Indian Association formed in 1883 to Indian National Congress in 1885, under whose leadership the opposition to the bifurcation of Bengal in 1905 was spearheaded. Later it led to the formation of two factions within the Congress Party – Naram Dal (the moderates) led by Gokhale and the Garam Dal (the extremists) led by Tilak. A large number of revolutionaries and the Azad Hind Fauz (army) led by Subhash Chandra Bose contributed to the freedom movement according to their policies and available resources.

He further elaborated on the circumstances under which Lokmanya Tilak emphasised that 'Freedom was our basic right' and how in 1929 at the Lahore Congress Jawahar Lal Nehru declared 'Total Freedom', how Mohandas Gandhi left Africa and returned to India to lead the movement through non-violent means, beginning his movement from Champaran, a part of Mithila, which has culminated today in the declaration of 'Quit India' movement and 'Do or Die' as the final call. He stressed that the time had come for India to attain freedom; no one could now stop that. Sooner than later the British will have to leave our country.

People were regularly clapping during Manikji's speech. Clapping had also taken place when Annie had entered the school premises dressed in an Indian sari and sporting a large red *bindi* on her forehead.

When Annie stood to deliver her part of the speech after Manikji's was over, there was a large sonorous clapping from everyone present there. Everyone respected her like Manikji.

In her speech, Annie supported Manikji's views about Independence and emphasised that India, which possessed such a large repertoire of ancient literature and equally ancient culture, could not be ruled by outsiders for long. She strongly supported the principles of Truth and Non-violence as Mahatma Gandhi practiced and considered these as the best weapons by which many wars could be won around the world and finally would lead to the welfare of the people at large. She further added that these principles would become the guiding light for the future generation. Only then there will be peace and prosperity in the world.

During her speech and at the conclusion there was a loud applause from all the corners of the lawn. Her speech was in Hindi but even though not fluent, everyone understood what she had to say.

After Annie, Abdul Khan also gave his scintillating speech in Maithili which was greatly appreciated by the assembled crowd.

The meeting ended by sunset but people remained on the lawn, in small groups discussing the action plan and other small matters etc. Slowly they began to return home. Some people also came towards Manik Jha and Annie and discussed the situation for a while. People expressed their appreciation for the speakers and finally, after the usual parting greetings they began to disperse.

Now it was getting darker. Annie's *sampani* cart was parked outside the school gate. Turning towards her, Manik said, "Your tea time is getting late. My house is close by. Why don't you come there and have tea? My father is unwell."

"Panditji is unwell? You never mentioned that. Now I shall certainly go and visit him". She instructed the cart driver to slowly follow her and both of them began walking towards

Manik's house. A few people, who had been in the last batch with them, also accompanied them.

At the *dalan*, Panditji was on his bed as usual. The two chairs were kept in front of his cot and on the other cot three old men along with Shastriji were sitting and talking in low voices. The lamps were burning at their usual places and the *lotas* were kept near each of the cots.

As soon as Annie took her seat after she paid Panditji her respect, he expressed his surprise, "Today you have come alone, where is Jennie?"

-"Some guests from Purnia including her mother and sister have arrived. She is busy taking care of them."

Annie did not tell the actual reason.

For some time she talked about Panditji's health and then about the Independence Movement. After a while, the people who had come from the meeting with them left. Only the old people remained.

Tea and toasted bread along with a glass of water arrived for Annie. Manik took tea only.

Taking leave of Panditji and the other elders present there when Annie began to return to her Bungalow, Manik accompanied her. On the road where her *sampani* cart was standing, she told him to return as it was getting late.

-"You must be very tired", Manik said, "Please get into the cart. I shall accompany you further for some distance."

-"It is very dark. You will face difficulty on your way back."

-"I have taken a difficult path, what's the worry then?"

Annie asked the cart driver to drive along slowly and she followed the cart on foot with Manikji. "Some of the difficulties are your own creation", she said.

-"Like what? The social-political path?"

-"No, many have taken to this path; this is the call of the hour for every Indian. I am talking about your personal affairs. How old are you?

-"I may be in mid-forties, why?"

-"In our England people get married till the age of seventy-eighty. Considering that you are young...."

-"Look", Manik cut her short, "England is England and India is India. Even though human emotions might be similar in both countries, the traditions and social customs are entirely different. Even if in England or for that matter in the entire Europe, many things may be happening, those are not possible in India, certainly not in the upper strata of the society. My Brahman community, in particular, is very conservative. I cannot say what will happen in future, future is unknown."

-"You have begun lecturing again. All these things I also know now to a large extent. Can I ask you something? ... Okay, leave it for now, please return back. It is quite dark."

-"I am not at all afraid of darkness. Recently I was not regular at the school, was mostly away and very busy at the same time. I am meeting you after many days. It feels nice to walk in your company. Shall I say something? Oh no, you wanted to ask me something.

-"Not now, first tell me what you wanted to say."

-"Nothing special."

-"Even then..."

-"You looked wonderful today when you entered the meeting ground."

-"Anything special?"

-"Can't say exactly. I'm not able to find a suitable word. Just your look at that time and how I felt... It is still etched in my memory. I can see it before my eyes even in this pitch-dark night."

-"You can see me in dark?" Annie was pleased to hear this. "Even now?"

-"Darkness has never been a barrier. I can see you much more clearly when I am alone and close my eyes."

Annie suddenly stopped; she could not control her emotions. She took hold of Manik's hand and said, "Surprising, exactly this happens to me as well. In my solitude, I see you very clearly when I close my eyes."

Manik felt great pleasure in holding each other's hand and standing so close together in the darkness. No one was speaking anything. But both minds were filled with terrible storms of strong emotions, words and experiences; storms which were fighting hard to come out and express.

Manik was the first to overcome the storm. He saw that the *sampani* cart had already gone a little distance away. He said softly to Annie, "Your cart is going away."

Annie slowly released her grip over Manik's hand and taking a deep breath, said, "Please do return now."

-"Why? Do you want to get rid of me?"

-"Manikji, please don't tease me. I guess I'm right. Even then I can walk with you for miles even in this darkness; rather I shall love to do so. ... Now I implore you to come with me to the Bungalow, have a cup of tea made by Roopy and then only return. My *sampani* cart will take you back."

Both of them began walking again.

The cart had not gone very far. Although Manik and Annie had been talking in English, which the cart driver was not able to make out, he felt he had left them far behind as he couldn't hear them talk any more. He stopped the cart and when he found the two within hearing distance, he began driving the cart slowly as usual.

-"Thank you for your offer", Manik said, "But you know no matter how late it is the night, I never take the help of anyone while returning home.... And again, why did you have to specify that tea would be made by Roopy? You know the Gandhians are against untouchability."

-"I know. Now don't be serious. Don't I have the right to tease you? Even then I beg pardon for the lapse. ...Now, go ahead and tell me what you wanted to tell about my entering the meeting ground."

-"Forget it, nothing serious."

-"Whatever it may be, you have to tell. Can't we share our pleasures?"

-"Why not? I have never kept anything secret about me. Actually, I had seen you after a long interval. I saw you dressed in a sari, sporting a large red *bindi* like a typical Indian woman. You looked simply gorgeous. I felt as if after a long journey through a desert I had reached an oasis, full of greenery and shade. It looked to me as if the Moon was slowly appearing after piercing through a dense cloud and shining brilliantly. Or one could describe my feeling then as if a fairy had just descended from heaven and slowly walked towards the stage at the meeting venue."

-"Oh, please stop. I am nowhere near such a great imagination. Please do not exaggerate." Annie enjoyed listening to Manik's praise in poetic language, she was thrilled and gratified, but for the sake of formality, had to tell him to stop.

-"You will never know what you are. Only I know. I am telling you the truth, when I saw you the first day in Sari, I can't describe how I felt. And today when I saw that red *bindi*, I felt smitten."

-"Smitten? Okay!"

-"I will tell you later. We have arrived at the gate of the Bungalow."

Bahadur, the security guard, had opened the gate already. A few orderlies, some bouncers and a bearer were already waiting there.

All of them were surprised to find that the *sampani* cart was empty and Manik Jha and Ma'am were entering the gate on foot. They all saluted them.

Petromax light was kept ready there. In the dining hall, Peterson and other guests were having dinner. Drinks were being served to the guests among chit-chat over dinner.

Annie straightway entered her room with Manik. Manik sat on the chair and she sat on the bed.

-"You must be very tired, it seems." Manik said with a smile.

But before Annie could open her mouth, Jennie appeared and answered, "So long as she is with you, she will not get tired", and she began laughing.

From her way of speaking and the smell coming from her mouth, both Manik and Annie guessed that Jennie was drunk heavily, even though in general she had quit drinking.

-"O wicked dame, you are always spying on us." Annie teased her sister-in-law.

-"What can I do? I feel lonely without you. It was getting late and we all were worried. Your brother was also worried and on his prodding, I kept checking every few minutes if the occupant had arrived. Just now when I saw you, I ran towards this room. I saw you with Manikji. All my worries were gone then and I was pleased at the same time."

Jennie turned towards Manikji and said, "Many thanks to you that you brought your Annie safely to the Bungalow. I have also not met you for a long time. What will you have?"

Both understood the implication of 'your Annie' as stated by Jennie. They also realised that Jennie was not saying in jest or satire but expressing her simple humorous affection towards both of them. Both of them smiled at Jennie which showed their tender feelings towards her.

-"You have taken a lot of drink today." Annie questioned.

-"Please modify your statement my dear sis-in-law. I have not taken a lot of drink; rather I have been forced to take a lot of drink." Jennie smiled and continued, "After many days, I was caught by your brother and that too in front of all the guests. In spite of my best entreaty, he did not agree. And he forced me to drink. What could I do? I was helpless. During the day I have to listen to you and during the night he is the master. I face such a treatment all throughout the day."

-"Jennie, the drinks have gone to your head and you have become very talkative. Will you only keep talking or ask us for some tea?"

Roopy entered just then as if she were waiting outside and listening to her call. As earlier she touched the feet of Manikji in reverence and then telling them that she would bring tea, left the room.

-"Have all the guests finished their dinner? What about your mother and sisters?"

-"They are at it, and the party will continue for a while."

-"Are you required there? You were also taking dinner, please go and finish that."

-"Actually I have finished my dinner. But I shall join you and take a few slices of bread. Let me go and prepare. I know Manikji will not take anything else."

And she left in a hurry.

-"Yes, you did not tell me."

-"What?"

-"The story about your emotions, seeing me in sari and a red *bindi* and your feeling smitten."

-"I see that you do not forget anything."

-"How can I forget your words, that too so pleasing?"

-"Okay, let's forget it for now. More so, if they are harmful and dangerous."

-"It is not the question of dangerous or benign. The question is about the feeling. That can be judged only after listening to it."

-"It's not that serious a matter. Just telling you to quench your inquisitiveness. Seeing you for the first time in sari I felt that I should tightly embrace you. And today seeing a large red *bindi* on your forehead, I had a strong urge to kiss you." Saying this, Manik sank into a sort of melancholy mood with a wry smile.

Annie also became sad and pensive. She asked, "And you wanted to commit this in public. As you could not have done in public, so you suppressed your emotions on both occasions."

-"Please think over, Annie. Psychology aims to read the human mind. But it remains an attempt at best. It's almost impossible to reveal the mind in its entirety. Mind is an ocean — vast, dark, deep and impossible to see through and through. Which wave of thought will overtake it and when is hard to predict.... India is not England." Manik remarked with a smile, "A lot of things remain outside the public domain here. I am sure you would have noticed it yourself."

-"You could have fulfilled your desire in private", remarked Annie.

-"Look, the emotion arose at a public place, that's why it suffered a setback. I will have to recall whether such an emotion ever arose in private at all." Manik replied with a grin.

-"If you ever recall, please do tell me." Annie also grinned and focussed her attention on the matured but handsome face of Manik, who wore an inestimable perseverance of unconquerable willpower. His eyes were glowing with simplicity and his lips wore a sweet innocent smile.

Feeling the gaze of Annie, Manik was a little unsettled and began looking out of the window in darkness.

Annie's heart was filled with unprecedented reverence towards Manik. She felt him very close to her.

By then Roopy entered with tea and the bearer with the eatables. Jennie also entered with the news that the dinner party of the guests had come to an end.

Manik got up after tea and said, "Let me go and say goodbye to Peterson." All the three left together.

In a surprising move, everyone in the dining hall got up to greet Manik. Manik said to them, "Please be seated. I just came to say goodbye to you all. ... Peter, Annie had gone to a meeting at the school. After the meeting, she went to my house for a cup of tea and also to inquire about the health of my father. I am responsible for the delay that caused you to worry. Please forgive me for that. I came here accompanying her for safety and also to have a cup of tea."

-"Not my tea, but Annie's tea." Peterson replied in jest.

-"But you are the Master of the Estate now."

-"No, Annie is elder."

-"Peter, this shows your regard and affection for your sister. But the reality is that since olden days our society the world over, in most parts, has remained patriarchal."

-"So do you consider us and yourself belonging to the same society?" Mr. Johnson quipped suddenly. "If so, then why are you people trying to drive us away from this country? I request you to sit down for a while among us here." And Mr. Johnson stood up from his chair.

-"Thank you", Manik said to them and took his seat on a vacant chair. Others also sat down. Everyone was eager to listen to Manik's reply. Peterson gestured to the bearer to clear the tables. A couple of servants came to assist him.

-"See Mr. Johnson, long ago we all had lived together, belonging to the same society and rather the same family. Hence the guiding force was Mother, which is central to all the languages and cultures. This was clearly stated by none other than Sir William Jones. ... Later people dispersed to different regions. People forgot that they belonged to a common lineage and familial bonds. Even if some did remember, circumstances made them inimical to each other. That led to fights among societies and countries which have resulted in so much unrest. The ongoing world war is a direct result of such a clash. ... There was a world war earlier too. Both these wars originated on the European soil. .. Now take the case of England. .. Earlier a tribe named Briton lived there. Later other tribes joined and the ensuing struggle resulted in Anglo-Saxon race. That's why the entire land was called Britain and a smaller region was named England. ... But what happened in India? Here from approximately ten thousand years before Christ till about five centuries later, many tribes from different places came, settled and merged into a single society and civilization. Everyone today is an Indian whose motto is tolerance and co-existence. That's why the Indian society's ideal is *Vasudhaiv Kutumbakam*, the world is a family. All of us have only one wish: *Sarve bhabantu sukhinah*, Everyone should be happy."

Manik paused for a moment. Everyone was listening in rapt attention. Every face displayed respect towards Manik. They had become pensive. They felt it was he who saved them from any harm and stopped all violence in the morning.

The atmosphere was quiet. Manik had cast a magic spell on the listeners. Jennie and Annie were particularly pleased with this effect.

The bearer, Roopy and the orderlies, standing aside, were also pleased even though they did not understand what Manikji said. They could observe the feeling of respect displayed by all.

-"Then why this call for Quit India today?" Mr. Johnson was not yet satisfied.

-"Mr. Johnson", Manik began with a wry and sarcastic smile, "I know you for a very long time. You and Mr. Kutt came to India almost simultaneously, mainly for trading purposes. In the beginning, you people did some small-time trading, it's true. But later by some manipulation and dishonesty towards your own employers, you people became landlords, by hook or by crook. You constructed sprawling Bungalows and began living here like Lords in England. ... Exactly in the same manner, Robert Clive also came and began his tyranny. Since then until the time of Warren Hastings, tyrannical rule and exploitation of the resources continued which only fuelled the Industrial Revolution in England. Even during those days, there were some sensible people who had spoken against the exploitation and Robert Clive had to face litigation for a long time. I am sure you know these events."

-"Yes, I do." This was the sudden outburst from one of the guests, a friend of Peterson, who had arrived from Calcutta. Both Mr. Johnson and Peterson looked at that person with angry eyes but keeping the decorum, said, "Yes we do know these events".

-"When you know these then certainly you would not have forgotten more recent ones, the shooting by General Dyer on unarmed civilians who had assembled at the JallianwalaBagh to celebrate their annual festival. You must know that in this case also, there was strong opposition to Dyer's actions and many had condemned him. I should, however, add that during this period public services like trains and postal facilities did come into existence in this country which was advantageous to the local population. In fact, you must agree that even these services were more to help the Government run their machinery smoothly and carry out repressive acts. You cannot deny that during those years our country faced severe drought in many places for several years at a stretch which killed a large population of this country. Gandhi has come to oppose the Government and their style of functioning which is responsible for such acts, through non-violent means, a unique experiment. In this fight, no one is expected to use any weapon, least of all to harm any British or the other Government servants. It is a different matter that there are other elements fighting for independence that do not subscribe to the Gandhian philosophy of Truth and nonviolence. We have no enmity with any particular class or tribe, be they the British or others. We are opposed only to the ruling system. Our aim is to immobilise the Government machinery so that they quit India. You have seen today only the British flag was lowered, which is symbolic of British rule, nothing else was done. I can also add that any individual, be it Mr. Johnson or Peterson or anyone else, can stay in this country as an Indian citizen, or even as a foreigner, after the Independence is achieved, so long as they respect the Indian rule of law."

-"I personally want to thank you, Manikji, that no damage was done to our property here." Peterson expressed his gratitude.

-"In reality, this expression of gratitude is to the Gandhian principles, which I accept as one of the soldiers."

-"Gandhi is not only relevant for India", the same young man from Calcutta said, "but for the entire world, that's my opinion."

Mr. Johnson and Peterson did not like this statement. But Manik's arguments had been so forceful and logical that everyone had to accept that, no one dared say anything against them.

-"Mr. Johnson, you are senior in age and respectable to me also. If any of my statements have hurt you, although that was certainly not my intention, then forgive me. I have bored you with my monotony, my apology again." Saying this Manik got up.

Everyone got up suddenly.

-"Pandit Manik Jhaji, I know you will not take dinner here, no matter how much I press you for that. But I have a special request..."

-"Mr. Peterson, I have already accepted your request, just a few minutes ago, on the insistence of Annie and Jennie, I took a few slices of bread and tea. So I have fulfilled your request. .. As far as dinner is concerned, since I am within your Zamindari, every grain belongs to you; it does not matter whether I eat here or there. Even then I must thank you for the invitation. What is your second request?"

-"My only request is that since it is quite late in the night now, I urge you to take the *sampani* cart to go to your house."

-"Thank you for the offer. Rest assured I have no fear moving around within my village at any time of day or night."

Saying this, as Manik came out of the hall, the young man from Calcutta, approached him and said, "Pandit Manik Jhaji, I was immensely impressed with you on this trip to this village. I am myself deeply devoted to Gandhian thoughts. Thank you very much." He extended his hand, which Manik took and shook it.

-"You stay at Calcutta and study there. I am also delighted to meet you. You are making a true evaluation of Gandhian philosophy. What's your name?"

-"Albert Dyson." He said politely.

-"Thanks, you must be aware that there is the Royal Asiatic Society in Calcutta founded by Sir William Jones. You will get a lot of material on Indian culture and ancient Indian literature there. You can ask anyone to guide you."

-"I know, I am a regular visitor there. I met a strange person named Robert Pincot there..."

Suddenly everyone turned around. Many voices asked in unison – "Robert Pincot?" Annie's voice was particularly loud.

-"That very rogue and vagabond Pincot?" Mr. Johnson sarcastically commented.

-"You are right Mr. Johnson. I have also heard that his past history was like that. But now he is a completely transformed person. He has become a perfect Indian saint. Not only has he left meat and drinks, but he has taken to dressing like a saint here and even wearing a wooden sandal. He is always absorbed in his studies. He hardly goes anywhere. His fame has spread far and wide. Anyone in Calcutta and Bombay, who wants anything to know about India consults him. Among the scholars, in particular among the Oriental Scholars, his name is taken with great reverence. He is at present working on ancient Indian literature. He only motivated me towards Gandhi and is helping me to understand the works." Albert Dyson narrated all in a single breath.

-"He used to frequently visit us here earlier." Peterson added.

-"Very true. He narrated a number of stories related to this place, concerning Mr. Kutt, you and specifically Ms. Annie. He considers her as his Guru and reveres her always during his talks. I became interested in visiting this place since then. I must thank Jim for this that he permitted me to accompany him to visit this place and meet Ms. Annie."

At that stage he committed another strange act – bending forward like any Indian does, he touched Annie's feet and taking his hands to his forehead, saluted her with folded hands. He told her, "I have been waiting for this moment since the day before yesterday. Yesterday I went a couple of times to your room but finding you busy, I did not feel like disturbing you. I feel guilty that I could not perform the duty given by my Guru just after arriving here." Feeling shy, Dyson continued, "This Indian style of showing reverence was taught to me by my Guru. I shall again meet you tomorrow. And Pandit Manik Jhaji, my Guru has also mentioned about you. He respects you greatly. He advised me to talk to you. In addition, I have one more wish..."

-"What's that?" Manik was getting more and more curious about this person.

-"I want to visit all the places and kiss the earth there wherever Mahatma Gandhi has visited in this locality. As my Guru told me, you are the only person who can help me in this endeavour. We shall talk in detail later. Presently it is getting very late for you." Saying this he again paid Manik his respects in true Indian style.

Everyone was impressed and fell silent.

Annie felt overwhelmed.

Mr. Johnson and Peterson were too bewildered.

Manik took leave of all and left.

Peterson said to Dyson, "Let us go, I want to hear more about your Guru."

Everyone turned towards the hall.

But Annie and Jennie took the opposite turn and following Manik proceeded towards the gate.

"Oh, you two are coming here again? And who is the third – Roopy?"

"Yes, Roopy, she hardly ever leaves us alone, always follows us like a shadow. Actually, Annie has made her a companion. We met her just after coming out of the hall. We thought to make sure that you really 'gate out'." Jennie replied.

-"Why, are you people really so much fed up with me?" Manik smiled.

The faint light from the petromax at the gate was falling on their faces. Bahadur was waiting.

-"It seems you are more fed up with us. Otherwise, why would you people organise this 'Quit India' movement?" Jennie asked.

-"Jennie, no doubt you are extrovert, but also naughty. You very well know that this Quit India movement is neither against any individual nor even the British race. It is directed against the British Rule. You should learn something from Annie when you become her disciple."

-"Not going to, already am her disciple. But you better be careful with Annie. An extrovert speaks out whatever comes to her mind and hence she is clear and dependable but no one knows what a silent person thinks or will do at any occasion."

Annie lovingly pulled Jennie's cheeks and smilingly said, "Let us go, it's getting late".

-"Yes, it's getting late for your dinner also. Please go." Manik replied on his way towards his house, "But Jennie, in this Quit India movement, no matter who goes or stays, I shall not allow you two to leave India."

-"You will hold both of us." Jennie cut a joke, "Roopy had explained to us that you people have the custom of polygamy. But you have decided not to marry as I have learnt from Annie."

-"Why do you always connect the relationship between a man and a woman only through the lens of marital union? Can't we stay as friends?" Manik turned around and smilingly asked.

-"Both of you are talking nonsense", Annie commented.

-"Whose life is more useless than that of you two?" Jennie shot back. "No emotion, no action, nothing, bland. Anyway, let me change the subject and ask Manikji one question."

-"What?" Manik was alarmed.

-"Will you give a truthful reply?"

-"I always try to remain truthful and keep a distance from falsehood."

-"Then please tell me why did you not get married so far after the death of your first wife?"

-"Now the question is not relevant, I am past the age of marriage. Manik replied and began walking towards his house."

-"Manikji, I know Roopy told us that people even older than you have got married a second time in your society."

-"Oh, so you have been collecting all the information from Roopy. You are truly knowledgeable."

-"You are trying to divert the topic. But I am determined to get the answer from you. Is it not true that you have been pressured by your family for more than ten years now to get married again?"

-"You are right."

-"Is it not true that around the same time ten to twelve years ago, Annie also announced to remain unmarried?"

-"Possible, but Annie alone can confirm."

-"Annie does not have to tell anything. I know it and remember quite well."

-"So what is the conclusion that you draw from this observation?"

-"The conclusion is straightforward – both the decisions are interconnected with the resolve of both of you. I have told this to Annie also." Jennie clapped saying this.

By that time they had arrived at the main gate. The security guard Bahadur looked around hearing a loud clap. He opened the gate quickly. Roopy also did not understand because of language problems but she guessed something anyway looking at the smiles of Jennie. Manik and Annie cast a mysterious glance at each other and smiled.

Manik commented, "Jennie, you should have been with the Scotland Yard. You could have succeeded in getting confessions from hardened criminals."

-"You people are engaged in all useless talks till now." Annie said in exasperation, "This Albert Dyson fellow has turned out to be really a wonderful character. His wishes should be fulfilled."

-"That will be done, no doubt. I am also interested in visiting those places. But more surprising was the tale about Pincot's transformation, whose entire credit goes to you."

-"Do you have any doubt about that?" Annie smiled while saying this but Manik sensed a tinge of sarcasm hidden there. He commented, "After such a long time, why bring out the subject of a moment's weakness on anyone's part? But if you decide to continue, let me also add in jest that quite likely my weakness of that moment might be a true feeling, which could have great psychological significance."

-"That's exactly what I had told that day also that it was a psychological truth and that truth I liked very much which showed your profound commitment."

Both laughed with a sense devoid of any malice.

Roopy looked at them both laughing and was happy about the moment's discourse. But Jennie held both their hands and in a very childlike manner pleaded, "I did not understand anything: neither that 'momentary weakness' nor that 'psychological truth'. It seems there is a deep secret of some past event. I implore both of you to clarify otherwise I shall not get any sleep tonight."

Annie stepped in, "Jennie, let him go. I shall solve your problem during the dinner."

-"Good. Now in my absence even if you abuse me, I shall not come to defend. Okay, bye." And Manik crossed the gate and quickened his pace.

Bahadur closed the gate again.

*

Annie had finished her dinner. Roopy had made the bed, cleaned the table and gone to take her dinner. The faint inaudible noise coming from the dining hall area indicated that the guests had also finished dinner and were preparing to go to bed.

"Jennie", Annie said, "It is quite late in the night. It seems the guests are also tired and preparing to go to bed. You are feeling sleepy I can see. Please go and have rest."

-"But I am not going to leave you until you tell me the story of that 'momentary weakness' and 'psychological truth' related to the secret encounter between you and Manikji." Jennie smiled mysteriously.

-"Oh, you have still not given that up. ... But the curiosity you have about the incident, which you think is a 'mysterious encounter', is in fact nothing of that sort. It is just a reaction which Manikji erroneously called 'moment of weakness' in haste."

-"Whatever that may be, I expect you to tell me the entire story truthfully."

-"You naughty dame!" Annie said smilingly, "Actually neither there came any occasion nor was there any urgency felt about it. Otherwise, I should have told you long ago. In reality, the event relates to the period when Pincot used to frequently visit me. He was physically attracted towards me and here he used to get plenty of drinks as well. And you are well aware of his earlier impertinent behaviour which just a few hours ago Mr. Johnson had described."

-"Yes I know very well. He was always after young women." Jennie smiled.

-"In fact, he could never succeed with me, even though he tried his best. Somehow his courage failed in front of me. It is possible that he was waiting for me to return his advances. But I had developed a terrible hatred towards him. That might have led to his defeat. But he did come, sit near me. Once or twice he tried to get physical but was strongly rebuked."

-"When you hated him so much, why did you not tell him bluntly to not come at all? Why did you allow him to sit near you? You might also have left the place on some pretext or other."

-"But something about him attracted me."

-"Attracted?" Jennie became serious.

-"Yes, attracted because of his patience. That led me to try Mahatma Gandhi's change of heart experiment. First I began by telling him stories about India's past greatness. Then I tried to get him interested in Indian philosophy and literature. I was fascinated to see him taking interest on these subjects. He even stopped drinking with Peter and used to spend more time in my company. And ... one day he disappeared, which we all know. Surely you will admit Jennie that my experiment was a success."

-"That's how he regarded you as his Guru and sent his disciple Albert Dyson to go and pay respects to the Guru in purely Indian style."

Annie looked sharply at Jennie. She did not find any semblance of sarcasm or malice in her eyes. She then added, "He did not send him; you probably didn't pay attention to Dyson's statement. It was only when Dyson became conscious and decided to visit the Guru of his Guru, then only the question of salutation might have arisen and probably Pincot might have suggested him to adopt purely Indian style."

-"Annie, this Dyson fellow is also strange. So humble and disciplined."

-"Yes, that's why he took the journey to visit this place and also wants to see the places Mahatma Gandhi visited in this locality. You seem impressed. Do you have any plan to divorce my brother for this guy?" Annie said jocularly.

Jennie replied with equal jest, "First you think carefully over it and give your own suggestion. He is much younger to you and most likely a few years younger to me also."

-"What is my suggestion? It is the individual's choice."

-"Well, I may even leave Peter, but how do I leave you?" Saying this, she moved forward a little and embraced her. Releasing her grip she said, "Should I tell you something?"

Annie looked at her expectantly.

-"Even though your age has advanced, your beauty stays the same as in younger days. This provides a unique magnetic attraction to others but ..."

-"But what?"

-"The same posture doesn't permit any man to come very close to you or attempt sudden molestation, so much so that even Pincot could not muster courage. Later he even transformed himself. ... There is something more, particularly seen in the last few years."

-"What's that?" Annie smilingly asked, "You were never a keen observer of personalities."

-"It's true for my earlier days. But here your brother's aggressive and temperamental nature and your cool and composed company have transformed me too and made me sober."

-"Do you feel sorry for that?"

-"Certainly. Being sober is boring. It snatches away many pleasures.... But first listen to me..."

-"Go ahead."

-"That concerns people's views about you."

-"What do you mean?"

-"That's what I find about your personality having developed in recent years. The first feeling which arises in anyone's mind at seeing you is that of respect. Didn't you notice how Dyson saluted you with respect and humility? That did not have only his Guru's advice but his own internal submission to your personality."

-"But that should be taken as a good thing, no?"

-"Come on. If the attraction does not result in infatuation then what's its worth?" Jennie said with a twinkle in her eyes.

-"Infatuation? Does it really need to be so?"

Suddenly an unexpected thing happened. Heavily drunk Peterson entered Annie's room, was very surprised to find the two ladies in conversation. He addressed Jennie haltingly, "All the guests have gone to bed. I suggest you say good night to Annie and leave her to go to bed."

-"If only your sister leaves me, that I can come and join you. Please go, I shall join you shortly", Jennie replied to her husband. Peterson left the room.

-"Oh but I cannot leave without listening to that tale about Manikji." Jennie insisted.

-"Nothing serious, believe me. Actually during the days when Pincot frequently visited me, whenever Manikji would see me, a kind of jealousy would appear on his face. This is what I had told him a couple of times. That is all."

Jennie suddenly became grave and a bit sad. She took a long breath and said, "You missed something Annie..."

And she left the room.

Annie kept pondering over Jennie's words. What did she miss? She could find no answer. Whatever came to her mind, she quickly brushed that aside, "No, there was nothing to miss. Was it possible? What is unimaginable, impossible, what is there to miss about that?"

She went to bed but remained awake till quite late in the night.

The Year 1947

During the intervening period, the world has seen a lot of upheavals. A lot of water has flowed through the rivers from the Thames in England to the Ganga in India. So many times, floods came and receded. Political storms of many kinds engulfed the nations from Japan to the USA. The League of Nations formed after the First World War became the United Nations Organization after the Second World War.

Entire Europe was left in ruins, people were tired and numb. By the time the war was over, the economy of England was in shambles. The British had become poor on a global scale.

But India was no longer poor. With the combined effort of the rapidly growing Independence Movement and the liberal policies of the Labour government headed by Attlee, the growing eagerness of the Indian business community to rebuild the country through fresh investments gained momentum. The British Government had declared that they would make India independent on the 15th of August. Although India achieved independence, she suffered because of the Machiavellian policies of the British Government and the country was divided into two.

Preceding this declaration since last more than one year the talk of partitioning the country on religious lines, with the western and eastern parts together forming a new country, Pakistan, had gained momentum. Under pressure from the British Government, the Congress party, spearheading the freedom movement, had unwillingly agreed to partition. The creation of Pakistan brought untold miseries to humanity and suffering to people living along the border areas on both the western and eastern fronts.

The village of Dharampur also bore the brunt of partition, which had been living in peace and harmony within the jurisdictions of both the Purnia and the Bhagalpur Collectorates.

The large chunk of the western part of the village, populated by the Muslim majority, was merged with the District of Bhagalpur. In addition, small hamlets of the Muslim population were combined and became a separate Panchayat.

Over the last few years, the effort to create a separate Panchayat had gained momentum. Discord was also created among the populace in those hamlets on various petty issues, leading to several skirmishes, the destruction of crops of each other and litigations as well. Finally, with the combined effort of both the Collectors, the new Panchayat was given shape at the fag end of the British rule. They were being assisted in their design by Mr. Johnson of Raniganj, the erstwhile Indigo growing Landlord and through his efforts, also by Mr. Peterson.

Both Mr. Johnson and Mr. Peterson were frustrated at the news of the British Government's announcement of Indian independence. They were stunned. It was a complete setback for them.

But soon they gathered their thoughts and began planning to wind up their business in India. They planned to go to Purnia, then to Calcutta, from there to Bombay and then straight to England. Ah, what a comfortable and enjoyable life they led here in India! No matter it was the result of many falsehoods, injustices, cheatings, exploitations, and oppressions. They built palacial Bungalows and led a life in their youth like the Lords in England. Mr. Johnson had grown old enjoying all the pleasures. What a pity that he will have to go back to England at this age!

In England, Johnson's and William Kutt's forefathers lived in the same village. Johnson's forefathers used to work as cobblers and Kutt's family had been washermen. In their adolescent days, both William Kutt and Johnson had even committed several petty crimes including pickpocketing.

And that's when a team of businessmen had been sailing to India. These two young men had begged the party to take them by offering their services for any sort of menial jobs at sea and also later. That's how these two arrived in India directly at Calcutta. There they got employed by the Nelson Company having business in British textiles. They accepted the job to gain some foothold in this country. From Calcutta the Company sent Johnson to Ranigunj and William Kutt to Dharampur Pargana to hawk the British-made textiles around the villages, carrying the bundles on their shoulders.

Both Johnson and William Kutt used to meet each other at times. During one such meeting, they decided to cheat the Company and use the fund to start their own business in those localities. The business prospered, the capital multiplied and both of them became influential persons. They began sending gifts to the wives of the Collectors of Bhagalpur and Purnia. And they won the hearts of both the Collectors' wives.

That resulted in both of them getting permission to begin Indigo cultivation, a very profitable enterprise at that time. With the help of the Collector, large tracts of land were allotted to them at throwaway prices. The rent was fixed by the Collector. The Government had a better income from Indigo farming than smaller businesses conducted earlier by the two.

The profits also helped William Kutt (distorted as Kutta, which meant dog in the native language) to become a Sahib. With exploitation and loot, he amassed a sizeable wealth, expanded his Zamindari and also succeeded in acquiring the Bungalow built by a Frenchman in Dharampur.

Johnson had also prospered similarly in Raniganj.

The day arrived when Johnson sold all his properties at throwaway prices to Indian businessmen who could arrange ready cash and came to Purnia with his family. He kept the family under the protection of Collector of Purnia District and travelled to Dharampur to meet Peterson.

Peterson had also decided to return to England. He had likewise sold all his properties to whosoever could offer ready cash and was all set to leave for Purnia the next day.

The only person in Peterson's family who was not ready to leave India was Annie. She was attached to the country and her school very much as well. Finally after a lot of persuasion and imaginary threats of mistreatment of the British by Indians, she relented. Nonetheless, she was extremely sad for the last several days.

She felt as if she were lost in some strange land. She could not reconcile the loss she would suffer by leaving India for good. She would stare absentmindedly at things around her. She would stare at her peons, bearers and the *sampani* cart drivers without talking to them. She had no courage to talk to them lest a flood of tears would come out of her eyes.

Even though everyone in the house was busy preparing for the departure, she never missed going to school. But she is hardly her old self there, with vacant looks and a sad face. Manaikji is not around. He has gone to Patna to attend to some work of the Congress Party. Every footstep sounds as if Manikji has returned to meet her. She asks herself, "When will Manikji return?" At the time of leaving for Patna, he had promised to be back sufficiently in advance to see them off to Purnia. But he is not to be seen. No one has any clue either. Will she never meet him now? The thought frightened her terribly.

She had tendered her resignation yesterday. The school had organised a farewell for her. The school has undergone considerable change by this time. There are good number of students and also sufficient teachers – a sign of an established and prosperous school.

The former Headmaster, Pandit Trilochan Jha Shastri passed away some years ago. During the farewell ceremony, Manikji was absent. Mohan Mani is nowadays mostly in the Congress Party Headquarters, Sadakat Ashram, at Patna. Whole ceremony was a dull affair. Some of the older teachers did speak about Annie's sacrifice and her dedication towards the school. Those words were very touching and tears came out of her eyes. Everyone was grave and sad.

A large crowd of teachers and students had accompanied her at the time of leaving the school to her Bungalow. The crowd also had several people from the adjacent 'Tolas'.

Of late she has been roaming around many Tolas of the village with Roopy as her companion. She came across a large number of poor and deserving families, for whom she had recommended to her brother some favours. People from those Tolas would join the send-off party and would go back only after long persuasion. Everyone was in a sad mood.

Today again, as if by habit, she began getting ready for school at the appointed time. Roopy entered her room and was surprised. She questioned, "You told me that yesterday was your last day in school and you would not go there any more. So do you want to go there?" She felt ashamed and realising her mistake, replied, "Oh no, I completely forgot about that." And then she again was surrounded in a great despair. She began looking at things around her with vacant looks. After some time she lay on the bed and oblivious to her surroundings, stared at the ceiling aimlessly. She lost track of time.

In between Roopy came a few times and finding her in that condition returned. She herself was feeling very sad now. Her very dear and loving Mistress Annie would be gone to a faraway land and she would never meet her again in this life.

Annie has arranged for her a piece of land for the house and another five *bighas* of cultivable land through Peterson's intervention. Such arrangements have been done for all the servants, including the bearers, watchmen, Marshals, peons, valets and even the Munsi and the Managers. The entire workforce is in a sad state. Whatever the excesses of Peterson, they had overall enjoyed a life of plenty and protection.

Jennie also came thrice only to find Annie staring vacantly at the ceiling. Lastly, she had to disturb her. She came close, sat on the bed, touched her with tender hands and said, "Everyone has finished lunch. Now only three of us, you, I and Roopy, are left."

Annie replied in surprise, "Is it so late? I did not realise it. Please tell Roopy to bring lunch."

By the time Annie came out of the bathroom, lunch had been laid at the table.

While taking lunch, Jennie recounted, "Like you, I was also born here in this part of the country. Although I went to Calcutta for studies and to Bombay, Madras and some other places for tours etc., all my childhood memories are always from this land. I also developed so much attachment with this land that just a thought of leaving this place for good gives me pain."

Annie did not speak, just looked once at Jennie and continued eating with her head hanging down. She could not speak anything fearing an emotional outburst.

Looking at Annie's condition and her attachment to the school, Jennie had even proposed to Peterson to let her continue for some more years in India. The Bungalow would be there and a small set of servants for her needs so that she could attend the school. She could join them later in England.

Peterson had replied, "But how will she come alone? At the moment several people are going to Calcutta and Bombay. Some years later who knows what will be the condition here in India? And most importantly, the Bungalow, along with the Williams Market, has already been sold. We shall have to give possession of these properties to the owner soon."

That had made Annie even more sad. Even the last straw had been lost. She behaved totally absentminded and withdrawn.

Jennie knew what was going on in Annie's mind. She herself was sad about the whole situation. As if to console her, she said, "Some time ago, I had sent the peon Sonu..."

"Peon Sonu", Annie's attention was brought back, "Where to?"

-"To Manikji's house."

-"Why?"

-"You have been telling for the last two days that he has not yet returned from Patna. Just to inquire whether he came back. He had not returned at least till about half an hour ago."

-"Oh, it seems we may not meet him before we leave for England. Are we really leaving tomorrow morning?"

-"Yes, the luggage has already been sent on the bullock carts to Purnia. We shall take the train from there to Calcutta. By evening two cars are expected to arrive from Purnia Collectorate. We shall travel in that car."

-"In the car? Where to? To Manaikji's house?"

It seemed as if Annie had been dreaming and suddenly woken up and asked that question. She was still not focused and said so absentmindedly, Jennie thought. She had sensed during the first question itself that Annie was not focussed at all, lost in her thoughts and hence she had been eating only the dry bread without touching the vegetables.

After hearing the reply from Annie about going to Manikji's house in a car sent from Purnia, Jennie could not control her laughter; she shook Annie's head to bring her to sense and laughed aloud. Annie could not make out why Jennie would laugh just like that. She asked, "What happened? Why are you laughing?"

-"Looking at your condition. You have been so lost in thoughts that you did not even realise what you were eating – just dry bread, no vegetables at all. And milk is left untouched."

-"Oh, yes, I have probably eaten too much bread. Let me have some milk." Taking the glass of milk in her hand she asked,

"Tell me what we were talking about. I had become distracted a bit and could not concentrate." And she forced a grin.

Jennie however became grave and serious, "As we have to depart early tomorrow morning, I have something lined up for this evening."

-"What's that?"

-"In the evening we shall go to Manikji's house."

-"Yes, yes, that we must do. Panditji is counting his last days. We shall pay to him our respects once for the last time, and we shall also discuss the work related to the Charkha Samiti with the widowed sister of Manikji and give them some suggestions for its smooth continuance.

-"And it is quite likely that Manikji may arrive by that time."

-"I don't have much hope though, but we are going there anyway."

Saying this, Annie got up.

*

Panditji is lying semi-unconscious on his bed on the *dalan*. He regains consciousness once in a while, looks around and then again closes his eyes. He was being treated by the village *Vaidya* (practitioner of Ayurveda) but on the insistence of Panditji, that has been now discontinued. He is now given Gangajal into his mouth several times a day and very seldom very little food too.

The veranda remains as it was with minor changes. As soon as Annie and Jennie sat on the chairs kept in front of Panditji's cot, the attending servant briefed them about the ailing Panditji's condition. Another servant continued rubbing his feet slowly.

On the cot next to him two old men were sitting. It was not the earlier gathering anymore. Some of the old men had either passed away or become incapable of walking. So the veranda was looking almost empty. The bed sheets were folded and kept at one end on two cots. Only when some guests arrived the sheets were spread on the cots. Similarly, the water pots were no longer there under all the cots. Just two pots, one under Panditji's cot and another in between the other two cots.

Some young and some middle-aged people came in between, looked at Panditji, touched his feet in reverence and left. The whole atmosphere looked gloomy.

Annie was downcast looking at so many gloomy faces. She had learnt on arrival that Manikji had not returned yet. It depressed her further.

Yet, she continued sitting there, looking at the gate once in a while. Jennie also did the same looking at the deserted path sometimes and throwing a glance at Annie at other times.

Suddenly Panditji opened his eyes for a brief moment, as usual, looked around and again closed them. It was clear that he did not recognise the two ladies sitting opposite him.

The sun was still shining, sunset being half an hour away. A servant came from inside the house and informed Annie that all the ladies connected with the Charkha Samiti had arrived and were waiting inside. Annie had organised this in advance.

Annie looked around once and signalled Jennie to get up. Both of them looked at Panditji for a little while and then after touching his feet left the veranda.

The servant took both the chairs to the inner quarters.

The inner quarter had four houses on the four sides, all neat and clean, all of them having wide veranda, in one corner stood the Tulsi plant on a platform and a bamboo pole erected nearby carried a flag symbolising Lord Hanuman.

In another corner of the courtyard, a couple of long mats were spread, on which were sitting the ladies from neighbouring families who had been engaged in spinning cotton using the Charkha. All these women wore Khadi saris, their faces being proud of the fact that they were now almost self-sufficient in clothes.

Annie and Jennie had encountered such groups several times in the past during their visits. Especially Annie, as she had been a visitor here since the day she had helped form the Charkha Samiti under the leadership of the widowed sister of Manikji and asked the women to use their spare time in spinning cotton thread on their charkha. She had encouraged them for this work in various ways.

It was the result of her encouragement that soon about a dozen Charkha Samitis were formed in different parts of Dharampur village. Centres were formed to train the women where such women from a cluster of nearby households would gather for collectively spinning. In addition, some newlyweds, who had difficulty in going out, got the Charkha delivered in their own house and made good use of it. Bundles of cotton thread spun by these women were carried by the menfolk to the Khadi Exchange Centre – *Khadi Bhandar* - where threads would be examined for their quality, classified, weighed, and entered in a book. When the quantity was found acceptable, one could exchange for its value a sari or two or even a Khadi dhoti or a shawl.

Annie had been touring the village for the last several years and was greatly pleased with the progress among the villagers. She would be amused to find the local *jugaad* – innovation - for her to sit; it consisted of either a low bathing table, small in size or an *okhal* placed upside down, with a piece of cotton or blanket placed over it as a cushion.

When she saw it for the first time, she became very curious about its use and examined it in every possible way. It was amusing to find what it was.

Similarly, when the local women had seen Annie in a Khadi sari and sporting a large red dot on her forehead for the first time, they had been equally amused. Her extremely fair complexion, hair-do and handsome face shone further with the red dot even from a distance. It was no longer a surprise. The entire village recognised her as such.

Seeing Annie and Jennie coming towards the courtyard, the women became momentarily happy but soon their faces were covered in gloom realising that it would be the last meeting and never again in their lifetime would they be able to meet the two ladies.

As soon as the two ladies sat on the chairs, the women present there became sombrous. Some of them began wiping the corners of their eyes with the end of their saris. After wiping their uncontrolled tears, the first to speak was the leader, the widowed sister of Manikji. She could just say in a mixture of Maithili and Hindi, "We have been waiting for long; Roopy came to inform us of your visit quite some time ago, in the afternoon."

Jennie and Annie also looked sad. Annie controlled her tears, wiped her eyes and spoke in Hindi mixed with some broken Maithili, "We were sitting outside by Panditji's bed. He momentarily regains consciousness after long intervals. ... No news of Manikji either?"

-"No, but he had told us that he would certainly return today. He knows that you all will leave tomorrow. Will you never come back here again?"

While saying so, tears again rolled down her eyes. She wiped her tears. The whole atmosphere was so sombre as if a daughter was being given a send-off after her marriage. A well-settled establishment was suddenly being uprooted.

Jennie also remained sad. She kept mum for a while, looking out with distracted eyes.

It was Annie who finally thought a way out of the somber atmosphere. She asked Manikji's sister, "Will you not treat us with the *Tilkora* fry today? Jennie also has come to enjoy that dish."

Everyone heaved a sigh of relief as if suddenly the cloud had dispersed and a bright sun had appeared in the sky. Suddenly there was a flurry of activity among some of the younger women. Someone ran to the backyard to gather fresh *Tilkora* leaves, others went into the kitchen to light the fire and some others began to arrange for the ingredients. Manikji's sister called the cook to take charge herself even though many younger women were ready to help.

By the time *Tilkora* and *Chiura* were fried and served, the Sun had set and darkness had engulfed the courtyard. Immediately lamps were lighted in all the rooms and a lantern was brought near the assembly. Lanterns were also being hung on all the verandas.

By now Jennie had become adept at eating the fried *Chiura* using her hands. As they ate, chit-chat continued about various aspects of spinning. Everyone assured her that there would be no break in that work as they had found a very fruitful time pass which made them self-sufficient for clothes.

-"Annie sister, will you continue wearing Sari there in your country? We hear that women dress there like what Jennie is wearing."

-"Certainly on special occasions, if not regularly. It is true people will find it strange to see such a dress."

-"No doubt it will look strange but surely you look wonderful in a Sari. You look very pretty in a sari, almost like a fairy."

Everyone began looking at Annie with happiness. There was a sense of appreciation and thankfulness in everyone's eyes.

Because of Charkha and the encouragement from Annie, the women had now no longer to depend on male members of their family for saris. They proudly wear the saris woven out of cotton threads they spin with their own hands. The weavers also are very much indebted to Annie and always praise her initiatives. Because of Annie several restrictions within the society have been relaxed and the newlyweds have been able to move out of their house and visit the neighbours. The petty quarrel among women, which used to be rather a pastime, has also come down to a large extent. Long live Annie.

But Annie became curious about the meaning of the word 'fairy', "Were Indian fairies really extremely beautiful? Was that the context used by Manikji once while praising her? ... Oh, how unfortunate of me, if I am not able to meet him before we leave for England!"

She used to steal a glance at the entrance of the courtyard if by any chance Manikji entered there. Jennie sensed her anxiety. They had finished taking tea by that time. Annie got up and said, "It is getting darker now and your household chores are waiting as well. It's better we leave. I shall remember all of you throughout my life. If I have committed any harm to any of you, please do forgive me for that. I shall try to come back at least once to meet you all."

Everyone stood in her appreciation and spoke almost in a chorus, "That will be really great. We shall eagerly look forward to such an occasion."

Jennie began thanking them, "I shall never forget your hospitality. The taste of the fried *Chiura* and *Tilkora* leaves will always linger on my tongue."

Everyone walked with the two ladies down to the edge of the courtyard, and with heavy hearts, they bid them farewell. Manikji's sister came forward and giving Annie a packet containing two new saris, said, "Annie sister, it is the tradition in Mithila to give a lot of items to the daughter who goes away after marriage to her husband's place. Sari is certainly one of them. There are two saris for you two. Kindly accept this from us."

She gave the packet to Annie and began wiping her eyes which had become moist. A lot of other women had their eyes wet and were seen fighting tears.

Annie was moved for a moment. But quickly she recovered, took hold of the packet and fighting her pain of separation, spoke briefly, "Thank you all. I shall always remember all these."

She could not speak further. She held Jennie's hands and quickly came out.

*

Coming to the *Dalan* again, she stopped to have a look at Panditji. She looked all around. The two old persons had left long ago. A servant was sitting close to his feet, gently stroking the sole. Another sitting near his head was fanning gently. The lantern was hanging in the eaves. Some people were working in the nearby threshing yard adjacent to the *dalan*.

Annie took a deep breath and quickly moved towards the waiting *sampani* cart. Just after Jennie got into the cart and she was about to board, she suddenly stopped.

Moonlight had spread around and she felt as if Manikji was approaching with quicker steps towards them.

Sampani stood there and also Annie by its side.

Within minutes she was sure it was Manikji. She felt as if some strange event had happened. She had got some missing gem after a week's restlessness and anxiety. It was as if a long-cherished treasure had been found.

Annie's heart began racing fast. She was overcome with excitement.

By that time Manikji had come closer. He was panting because of brisk walking. He could haltingly utter, "I am coming via Kothi. There I learned that you two have come here. I have come almost running to meet you. ... I had been thinking that as a last wish, we should sit down and have tea together. I also need to inform you that the cars supposed to be coming from Purnia have already arrived…. Probably you people plan to leave early morning."

-"Oh, is this the information you had to share that you came running?" Annie commented with sarcasm.

-"Yes, I wish a trouble-free and smooth journey back home for all of you. What else can I wish at this moment? But …."

By that time Jennie, thinking that the dialogue may be prolonged, tried to come down from the cart. But Annie told her to stay there and let the cart move slowly. She along with Manikji walked slowly behind the cart.

-"You wanted to tell something?" Annie looked at Manikji.

-"Annie, I got the point of sarcasm in your reply but you did not pay attention to my offer of having tea together for the last time."

-"Now like so many other wishes, this wish will also have to be kept aside for two reasons. First, that we just finished tea here in your house, and second, that you are so tired after having travelled from Patna all the way. That's why we don't want to take you all the way up to the Kothi. More so, because, you will not accept to come back in the cart."

-"But if I say I am not tired at all then?"

-"Not even then", Annie told firmly, "We are not so selfish, but leave that aside. Tell us why were you delayed in returning from Patna?"

-"Mohan Maniji suddenly fell ill for a couple of days and then there were so many meetings concerning the type and scale of celebration to be had on the 15th of August and added to that were the issue related to the Constitution. But frankly, my mind was always occupied with you and your journey. … At times I used to get nervous and then later on I became desperate to meet you. … As soon as Mohan Maniji showed some improvement, I rushed back. I was constantly worried whether I would be able to reach in time and meet you."

Annie was very pleased to hear these words, particularly to learn that Manikji had not forgotten her and considering his engagements with the business at hand, made very sincere efforts to return in time. She once again gave a penetrating look at him as if seeing him for the first time.

Manik also stood still and kept smiling. He was smiling because of Annie's pleasant and happy face looking at him, being happy to finally meet her at the time of departure, the last meeting for life.

-"I was also worried whether we shall meet you before our departure." And suddenly she did something utterly strange and unexpected. She had never become so impulsive. She caught Manikji's hands by her hands and said, "I have a wish. You had felt something special on seeing me in sari and again with the red dot on my forehead for the first time. You were not able to fulfil your wishes. But now promise me you will fulfil my last wish."

-"Promise?" Manik was confused not knowing what it meant. He was particularly concerned looking at the very emotional longing at her face and her trembling hands. In that state of utter confusion he said, "Then you also have to promise me… I also have a wish."

-"Wish? Tell me."

-"No, go ahead. First you raised the issue." Manik smiled again.

-"Should I express? Sure you will not refuse?"

-"Never. At a time when you are leaving for good, whatever is possible within my means I shall be more than happy to fulfill." He stated with evident determination and looked at Annie.

Annie, however, did not prolong the dialogue. Instead, she went closer to the *sampani* cart and asked Jennie to come down.

As Jennie came down, she walked back to Manikji, and holding his two hands, told Jennie, "You please preside as a priest; I am going to marry Manikji at this very moment. You will be the witness and holding our hands like a priest does, give effect to the solemn marriage."

-"Marriage and at this very moment?" Both Jennie and Manikji were bewildered. Both felt that the sky had descended to meet the earth at a very unusual and equally important hour in a completely unimaginable way. Both felt that all the seven seas had gone into hiding. And on top of that, the meeting of sky and earth had created such confusion that all the living beings were running helter-skelter. Not only that, they had lost their senses also. Because of the suddenness and unimaginable surprise, their throats went dry. Both of them just kept looking at Annie in utter surprise.

Annie repeated her resolve, "Please go ahead, no time to waste. Didn't you listen, Jennie, solemnize our marriage."

Still, Jennie and Manik were not able to understand what Annie said, which seemed coming from an insane soul. Both of them repeated their question agian, "Marriage and now, that too in the middle of the road?"

Manik had absolutely no inkling of what was going on in Annie's mind. Jennie gathered courage and said, "But both of you had decided to remain unmarried."

-"Yes, the decision had been taken under special circumstances due to various reasons. And today because of those very reasons and those circumstances, I am changing my decision. Do you have any objection?" Annie began smiling after saying as much and looked at Manikji.

-"Why should I have any objection if Manikji agrees? But let me remind both of you that tomorrow early morning we are leaving this village for good." Jennie was still confused.

-"I am aware of our departure and that's all the precise reason that our marriage has to be solemnised this very moment.

Manikji is also tired and he should go back and take a rest." Annie added with a smile.

-"I am not able to digest anything. Departure tomorrow morning and marriage here and now." Jennie could not bring her to believe.

-"Why do you connect marriage with the journey? A journey is a journey and marriage is marriage. … When I am in England, at least I shall not have the remorse that for want of a suitable match, I remained unmarried. Now I shall have the satisfaction that I did get married with a suitable match and can spend my life as a married woman. That is sufficient for me."

-"And what about honeymoon?" Jennie still wasn't convinced.

-"Oh my stupid sis-in-law!" Annie pecked Jennie and asked, "Can you explain what this kiss was about? Was it for a married couple? No. Similarly, honeymoon has nothing to do with marriage per se. That's designed only for the bodily pleasure of husband and wife, sort of a ritual to enter the mutually enjoyable and procreating world. But my proposed marriage is neither for bodily pleasure nor for social acceptance. It is just a meeting of two souls. That way, both Manikji and I will be able to retain our earlier status of celibacy and for our mutual satisfaction remain married too. Come, don't delay. Peterson must be getting anxious. I also have to arrange my belongings to be taken on the journey. And we should not hold Manikji hostage for long."

By now Manik had come to read Annie's mind and whatever he understood led him to regard Annie very highly. In reality, Annie was not a lesser mortal; she stood on a much higher pedestal that ordinary folks would not imagine to reach. He also realised that the concept of marriage Annie proposed was as unusual as it was closer to the truth.

Jennie did not make out anything but she was obliged to carry out the task Annie requested. She took both their hands in hers and let them touch and hold each other in the traditional Christian way. Then she said, "That's what you wanted, right?"

-"Yes, but that is the European style. This must be complemented by the traditional Indian style of marriage which is solemnised by applying vermillion by the groom onto the scalp between parted hairs of the bride." Saying this, she opened a small sachet concealed on her person, and asked Manikji, "You have to apply this vermillion as tradition demands to complete the process."

Manik's surprise had no limits. Still, to honour Annie's words, whom he did love from his heart, he took vermillion from the sachet and with trembling hands applied it between her parted hairs. Regaining some of his wit, he asked her smilingly, "So you had come prepared with all the necessities? You must have planned it well."

-"Yes, that's true. If by any misfortune today we had not met, I had planned to carry this sachet of vermillion all the way to England and keep it as a token of my marriage and I would have lived as a married woman. Now I am formally married. My wishes are fulfilled. Now please tell me what you want to say." Annie took the vermillion sachet from Manik's hand, kept that under her blouse and looked intently at him.

-"Do you plan to take this vermillion to England?" Manik asked.

-"Of course, I shall. But quickly please do tell me your wishes. All of us are getting late."

-"Then please carry this also." And Manik opened a sari from his shoulder bag and gave it to Annie. He gave one to Jennie also, and remarked smilingly that the priest as well should get some gift.

-"It seems your gifts were also part of a well thought out plan. We accept it cordially and with profuse thanks."

-"But I did not plan it the way you did, having brought vermillion with you for the special occasion."

-"At least for the moment it looks like so. While leaving your house, your sister also gifted us saris and on the occasion of this special marriage, you also did the same. This will remain an invaluable gift for the rest of my life. I shall keep this always under the pillow and shall feel your presence." Suddenly Annie's voice choked with emotion, she could not speak further. She just held Jennie's hand and bidding farewell to Manik, only said, "Please go home… you must be very tired…. I shall try to come back at least once to India if I remain alive…. I shall send my address with a letter…. Hoping to be in touch… goodbye."

And she quickly turned back and went towards the waiting *sampani* cart.

The cart moved, kept moving and slowly lost track as it sped farther and farther.

The cart had become invisible. But Manik felt as if the cart was moving on an unending journey and it would continue its journey till time immemorial and both Annie and Jennie would be still sitting inside the cart. He would be able to watch them till he could; Annie would never be able to go out of his sight, never at all. He still felt that way.

But hold on, what happened? Why did things become blurred? Oh, possibly because tears came to his eyes. He wiped his eyes and true, he began watching Annie wearing a sari and bright vermillion shining between her parted hairs, very much like any Indian bride… very attractive, beautiful, strange and beyond imagination.

He lost track of the time for how long he kept wiping his eyes and each time having a very clear view of Annie moving in the cart. When he felt his legs aching, he got back his senses.

He then turned towards his house.

Look! Surprising that Annie is going to his house on the *sampani* cart.

His steps became quick.

His breathing became fast.

His heartbeat also accelerated.

Acknowledgments

My heartfelt thanks to Sri Kedar Kanan, who suggested to me to translate this novel by Sri Mayanand Mishra. Credit goes to him for this work. It was through his efforts that Sri Bhavanand Mishra, elder son of the author, kindly gave his permission for translation without any financial obligations. I am grateful to Sri Mishra for this kind act. I am also grateful to Sri Kirti Nath Jha for carefully going through the manuscript and making useful suggestions.